Sequía!

Sequía!

[say-key'-ah]

A novel by Alan Cambeira,

author of the *Azúcar Trilogy*

Alan Cambeira

Sequía!
A novel by Alan Cambeira, author of the Azúcar Trilogy

iUniverse books may be ordered through booksellers or by contacting:

iUniverse
1663 Liberty Drive
Bloomington, IN 47403
www.iuniverse.com
1-800-Authors (1-800-288-4677)

ISBN: 978-1-4917-6898-3 (sc)
ISBN: 978-1-4917-6899-0 (e)

Library of Congress Control Number: 2015908206

Print information available on the last page.

iUniverse rev. date: 05/20/2015

Dedication / *Dedicatoria*

*Para Paulina, una gloriosa flor caribeña que
nunca se rindió a ninguna medida de sequía
espiritual ... que en paz descanse.*

For Paulina, a glorious Caribbean flower who never
surrendered to any measure of spiritual drought
... may you rest in peace.

Contents

UNO

"*Coño!* [Damn it!]," the old man said irreverently since from his perspective there was basically no question whatsoever; he was thoroughly convinced that the dryness was a perverted reality ... a reality working frantically in still-unclear attempts to cut off the easy flow of the customarily soothing and tranquil breezes that blew over his island. There was a certain nervous quietness in the suffocating air as the old man continued his incisive rant.

"*Pero eh fácil?* [But you think it's easy?] And at my old age? Can it be that I am truly surviving this hell? *Coño!* The empty thorns lacking water and continuing to pierce my old dry throat are just too damn much punishment for any sane human to bear. I can't even remember the last time it was so damn dry around here."

And it was true. Everybody was worrying seriously about the absence of the ever-so-sweet rainfalls that used to arrive regularly at this time of year. *Don* Anselmo was worrying about the absence of his feelings… the absence of perhaps an approving nod from the island's sacred spirits themselves. The old man was beginning to think that his own senses might be roaming around aimlessly and completely out of control.

"*Dónde está esa maldita lluvia?* [Where is that damn rain?] It used be that you could always smell it coming; but not so any more," don Anselmo wondered if this was how the gods were punishing the island. And for what reason? The gods seemingly were actually gleeful in afflicting the residents with the worst kind of dry spell ... *una sequía* [a drought] …four years straight it had been like this.

1

According to the tormented old man, not one single drop of rain was nothing more than the unwarranted vengeance being unleashed by a cadre of disgruntled ancestral Island gods. The once luxuriant foliage of the expansive *flamboyán* trees, for instance, with their normally delicate, crimson-colored blossoms covering almost every inch on these glorious tress, used to be a readily accessible and welcome camouflage against the blistering heat on any given day. Along with the exotic tropical splendor of the abundant leaves of the *tamarindo,* the *macaw,* the *guanábana*, the umbrella-like jackfruit and breadfruit trees, as well as the *guayába* groves with their respectively seductive, aromatic fragrances, all these perpetually lovely gifts of Nature's generosity have now become unsuspecting, helpless victims of this painfully unyielding *sequía* that now reigns over the Island. More and more, every living thing was turning an odorless, dull, unattractive brown color, losing little by little their previously tingling luster and vibrancy. With absolute certainty, everything in every direction was slowly withering away.

"*Por todos los santos.* [For the sake of all the saints]. I plead with humility for relief from this undeserved torment. As in the days long gone when we all worked like the condemned slaves used to do on the wretched sugarcane plantations throughout the *isla* [island] … but survived the daily assaults, brutal and cruel as they were." *Don* Anselmo remembered all too well. He remembered that, without fail, they all nevertheless depended upon the collective protection of their revered ancestral spirits. Thoughts of that special place -- Ginen-- where all the sacred spirits live permanently '*an ba dlo'* [deep underneath the sea]. These were the ancestral spirits that always gave the people untold comfort from the exploitation and abuse faced throughout those difficult days. *Don* Anselmo's powerful faith and uncompromising love for all those spirits never left him.

His beloved parents, *'que en paz descansen'* [May they rest in peace], had taught him to acknowledge forever all the ancestral deities so that they, in turn, would make Ansemo's path straight and correct. It was a puzzlement, therefore, that now these same deities seem to have forgotten the people.

"I call each of you regularly by your name: Ezili Dantò, Mayanèt, Ogou, Danbala, Gede, Papa Legba: why have you once again forsaken us? Now, all those beautiful gifts of Nature that were always at the core of my soul have lost their glow with this *'maldita sequía'* [damned drought]."

Dramatic evidence was everywhere. No longer are the leaves green; no longer are there the beautiful colors and the rich aromas smoothing the senses. There remains no doubt that everything around the old man is suffering a slow and unworthy fate, and he could not understand don't why. The *sequía* is the certain victor in this uneven battle.

"*Mwin gwin ginyin la pèn; sé oun lavi' ki rèd.* [Damn it! Life is hard; I share so much of your pain.] I can still hear these sorrowful words that I learned so long ago from my humble parents. My old comrade from those awful days, *doña* Fela, -- leaving us when she did to begin her inevitable final journey to the other side ---used to remind us constantly of this fact in moments such as now. ...*Doña* Fela always had a way of offering me that special kind of solace and relief from whatever anguish was feeling at the time. It was like those fond memories of tasting a piece of delicious black cane on a hot afternoon; that black cane was so soft and sweet and full of rich, think cane juice against my dry gums that I would forget the ugly brutality of working the cane fields. She was so wise and good ... always had a soothing answer for all of life's seemingly unsolvable puzzles. She no doubt would have an answer for this damn *sequía.*"

...As he closed his old eyes, he chuckled in sweet remembrance of his deceased comrade.

The fact that the old man had survived that hellish nightmare at all said much about the divine will of his hallowed ancestral spirits. He had never even once betrayed or distrusted them; he resolutely didn't dare to do so. Those had been difficult times indeed at *Esperanza Dulce* sugarcane plantation, especially during the height of sugar production and then at harvest time. How ironic that the name itself of the plantation, *Esperanza Dulce,* means 'Sweet Hope.' He actually held no remorse nor sadness that *Esperanza Dulce* has long been demolished to be quickly replaced by the Island's most luxurious beach resort in the entire Caribbean. And he reflected upon how he had survived it all. The gods knew what a faithful and true follower to all the *'lwas'*[spirits] the old man continued being ... since his parents had first introduced him, along with his siblings, to the island's sacred traditions. But at this juncture in his old life, he found himself daring to ask if this patience and loyalty was still being tested. Was it even reasonable to ask? What real alternative was there?

What other explanation was there for this *maldita sequía* now dealing the *isla* such a harsh and unfair blow? Were the gods definitively turning their backs on the island's inhabitants after so many long years of dutiful obedience? "I ask my tortured conscious if the gods themselves have grown weary of the task of protecting us over the years."

"Anselmo Toussaint Altagracia, born the youngest of four sons to Adeline Peña and Pierre Altagracia, had arrived at the century-old *Esperanza Dulce* Plantation soon after slavery ended throughout the Island. The Altagracias were among the first wave of *cañeros* [contracted sugarcane workers]. Anselmo's older brothers Alix, Justín, and Herson, along with two of his father's brothers, all lived in the *'batey'* [sugarcane workers settlements]. They all shared a tiny, two-room shack that had a zinc roof; the two rooms were separated for matters of privacy by a pitifully thin, cotton sheet. The naked, hard-packed dirt was our floor; crude straw pallets placed randomly around the floor were their beds. Anselmo remember having no lights, no potable water, no indoor plumbing, no sewage or drainage system, no school, no medical clinic of any kind. Yet, they survived that stinking shit-hole thanks to the hope they collectively had that the grace of the *'lwa'* would forever protect them. Only Anselmo's cherished Felicidad Bustamante, among the hundreds of folks who lived there, could boast that she alone had been there longer than anybody else; nobody knew exactly when she first arrived at *Esperanza Dulce*. There was another unforgettable and honored companion -- Lola Despestre, who became the young bride to older brother Alix. It was his brother Justín and Fela, short for Felicidad, of course, who gave birth to their only child, a girl they named Solange.

As the family grew in numbers, they all rejoiced as they witnessed Solange, while still just eleven years old, become the child-bride to a very special *'cortador'* [cane cutter] at *Esperanza Dulce*. The cutter's name was José Ferrand. As if a divine miracle from the gods, Solange and José produced an amazingly beautiful and adorable baby girl whose unusual skin coloring was the same as that of granular, unrefined brown sugar... in the Caribbean what is called *'azúcar morena.'* Everyone noticed that this peculiar brown sugar color of the infant girl didn't just disappear after a few weeks or even after a few months as she was growing up. That odd, yet beautiful color would stay with her throughout her entire childhood and beyond. When she left the *isla* to go live in far-away Canada, she still carried this same color that she was born with, only now much richer. That exotic tropical coloring captured the attention of everybody who met her. Her name was Azúcar Solange Ferrand.

Coño. The old man remember how so many things were strange and confusing to him back then. For instance, he recalled how it was never clear in his mind whether his hardworking, honorable parents Pierre and Adeline were

Haitian or Dominican... *'Domínico-haitiano'*... is what folks say today. This is often the agonizing fate of so many other folks of mixed heritage on the *Isla*. That unpretentious, yet very noble spirit reflected in the character of *'mis padres'* [my parents] was the same sparkling light that Anselmo always saw in the soul of one of the bravest and most idealistic residents of their community, Sonia Pierre, now passed on to the other side with the sacred spirits...*'an da blo.'* Sonia's departure was sudden and quite unexpected; a massive heart attack stole the fierce leader from the community when she was only forty-eight years old, leaving a huge void in the struggle for justice and equality for all the folks of Haitian descent living on the eastern side of the *Isla*.

Everybody remember when Sonia was maybe just thirteen years old; she had rallied her *domínico-haitiano* neighbors in the *batey* and defied authorities by organizing a large protest march to demand basic rights and fairness for all the sugarcane workers at *Esperanza Dulce* plantation. She even spent a day in jail while the local police threatened to deport her and her whole family to the other side of the Island-- although she had been born on this side of the river and knew nothing about her so-called 'native country' at the time. A few weeks after Sonia Pierre's death, the Dominican Supreme Court upheld an earlier law that was aimed at reducing the use of suspected fake documents-- thus prompting the government to confiscate or annul birth certificates of all those children long as any of us could remember, it used to be that many of the new arrivals from across the Artibonite River automatically were given work visas without question... *Nada de problema.* But now the authorities, for no valid reason whatsoever, simply refuse to recognize the legal status of these workers. *Don* Anselmo continues asking, who are the gods punishing with this *sequía?*

"So it is that I drift easily in and out of consciousness as I think about just who I am. Much like Sonia's family and so many more in similar circumstance, all the members of my father' side of the family were born in a nameless, remote corner of what everybody still calls *'la zona fronteriza'* [the border zone]."

For the longest time this isolated region has been referred to as *'La Tierra de Nadie'*... meaning 'no man's land.' Since the governments on either side of the Artibonite River never officially settled the nagging question regarding precisely which government has legal possession of this forsaken stretch of terrain, it therefore belongs 'to nobody.' To this very day with foolish talk about building high walls and electrified fences erected to control the unlawful entry into the country, there are actually certain points along the lengthy, uncertain border where a traveler can simply roll up his pant legs or a woman and lift her skirt to freely wade across the ankle-deep stream that separates the two traditionally contentious neighbors. More than a few border guards on patrol, if offered a satisfying amount of *pesos*-- will gladly allow unhampered passage to the other side without fear of arrest. "Who are the gods punishing now?" the old man again insisted.

Over the many years of natural human flow back and forth through the region, including very common cohabitation there, the social and cultural interchange has been one of easy and visible harmony, with the unsurprising consequence of intermarriage that has been the case with the two cultural groups. Anselmo suspected that his own parents had been part of this inevitability. He knew that his father had been the perfect example of this circumstance. Folks all around had the greatest respect for Anselmo's father; he was what people used to call a *'prèt savann'*-- 'village priest.' Even now in the rural areas, this individual is that deeply religious man who always is expected to recite from memory, not read, mind you— certain Catholic prayers before beginning any of the traditional folk ceremonies of *Vodou*. All in all, Anselmo's personal story is one that has a history heavily interwoven with threads of abundant fog, legend, and mystery ... much like the histories of nearly everybody on *la Isla*.

"I don't think the human landscape that I left behind in my own consciousness has been altered to any great degree. I don't think it can be changed; it is so gravely scared. And for me, there are still too many damn open pits containing many painful and cruel losses and many memories of both sadness and joy."

But now at this stage of the old man's long life, there is no way of knowing if these pits will ever be closed over and disappear altogether. Or maybe he is unconsciously refusing to allow that to happen. *'No estoy seguro'* [I'm not sure.] It's the same way that this *maldita sequía* is not allowing anyone to breathe properly. Why won't the gods make it go away and bring the sweet rains that they have been so accustomed to having... and need so much? *Coño!* Who is sure of anything these days?

DOS

Without the slightest doubt, there was the one departure to *'ad ba dlo'* that grieved the respected elder the most... more than anybody else did. In fact, this single departure devastated every living soul-- men, women and children living in the *'batey'* and that had everybody crying hard for many days and nights. It was the departure of the most venerated elder of the community, Anselmo's dearly beloved friend and trusted comrade, *doña* Fela. *'La maldita cana'* [damn sugarcane] had finally robbed the community of its most precious treasure. The pure low-down hatred of that *'hijo de puta'* overseer Miguel Montalvo refused to allow the *batey* residents even one full day from working in the fields so that they might mourn Fela in proper fashion. The old man could still hear himself crying at the time of his comrade's death.

"Kité mwin sél. mwin ginyin la pèn." [She is leaving me alone and I am in so much pain.] How her death had hurt deeply inside his soul. "Leave this filthy pit of human misery, *mi querida azúcar morenita,"* *doña* Fela said before taking her last breath, in the weakest voice possible for a dying woman. "But above all else, guard your heart because it is the wellspring of life itself. *La maldita caña* is the only true enemy with all its evil and deceptive sweetness; don't let it bring you down as it has done me. *'La hierba mala nunca muere'* [Weeds never die.] So, you must leave this wretched place before it's too late." With that, the revered elder took her final breath on this earth and prepared to travel across 'to the other side' in order to reside now with the sacred ancestors. It had been the wise *doña* Fela herself who would be intimately involved in astonishing efforts to monitor her granddaughter's future thoughts and actions. Old Anselmo remembered how one particularly dark,

rainy and starless night long ago, deep inside the forest, in the solemn company of his loyal comrades Fela and Lola, the trio had performed an ancient, secret ritual that most folks in the *batey* thought had been abandoned and totally forgotten.

"We didn't have a single regret about what we had done that night," the old man recalled saying years later. "I can't count how many times I felt defenseless in the darkest hours when things seem cursed by our gods.*'Tout komplis nam mizè nou.* [All of us are complicit in our misery]." And again it was the determined insistence and wisdom of *doña* Fela that the innocent little granddaughter, an inquisitive and truly exceptionally intelligent adolescent, be allowed to leave the *batey* for a place called Canada. The child's generous and compassionate benefactors Marcelo and Harold— despite what the community at the time saw as a wickedly unwholesome and unconventional relationship between the two young men– proved to be vitally instrumental in the arduous process of Azúcar's remarkable transformation. Everyone in the *batey* witnessed with genuine excitement and joy how the little girl with the 'strangely colored complexion' was converted miraculously into the unselfish and relentless champion of the Island's thousands and thousands of oppressed workers while at the same time becoming the extremely wealthy, highly respected and influential business woman that she is today. Even in the matter of meeting her future husband, Lucien St. Jacques, the tireless efforts of Marcelo and Harold were directly involved in bringing the dynamic young lovers together.

Just as the mystifying *sequía* has made the ground crack because there has been no rain for so long, so too has *don* Anselmo's conscious made him never forget that awful time when the *Isla* itself also shook and 'split wide open'. The destruction was widespread and far beyond horrifying: the government reported that there had been well over 300,000 dead; thousands of folks injured in the most sinister way; piles upon piles of heavy concrete converted into instant unexpected tombs; perhaps a half million or more families displaced; people living among a string of flimsy, tarp-covered structures forming what were later called 'settlement camps.' The *'bateyes'* of the past had offered far better shelter than these shameful excuses for houses. Than as if that wasn't enough punishment, the cholera epidemic that immediately followed killed well over 8, 000 souls and health officials feared that perhaps as many as 600,000 more individuals were infected soon afterwards. The country had not experienced cholera in over a century; it was affirmed that the disease would continue killing innocent folks for many years yet to come. It was far from mere rumor or speculation that the newly arrived United Nations' peacekeepers' from the remote country of Nepal-- which most residents had never ever heard of before-- had actually brought with them a particularly deadly strain of cholera. It was no secret that the poor sanitation at the peacekeepers' camp had been directly responsible for the deadly outbreak.

"*Carajo!* Even when we lived in the goddamn *batey,* everybody -- including the youngest children-- knew to never allow human shit to get into the nearby streams," one community resident had remarked in total disgust and anger.

"*Anonse, o zanj nan dlo!* [Oh Angels underneath the water], when is all this going to end? Without fail, that is what everybody always wanted to know.

"*Mientras que hay vida, siempre haya esperanza*" [As long as there is life, there is always hope.], *don* Anselmo said to as he recalled the days of his childhood when he and his brothers used to listen with silent attention as their soft-spoken, yet stern father always whispered to them. The phrase usually seemed to be uttered immediately following one kind or another calamity. The precise adversity need not have been of major consequence. Rather, it was simply whatever manner of unanticipated misfortune that fell upon either the individual soul or afflicted the entire community. *Don* Anselmo knew that it was *'esperanza'* or *'lespwa'*-- 'hope' in Spanish and Kreyòl, respectively that kept the community alive. It was most certainly the element of hope that had saved little Azúcar; everybody witnessed the girl's startling metamorphosis from the drab little caterpillar into the astonishingly radiant and regal butterfly.

The conversion was far from anyone's remotest imagination. Marcelo and Harold had been the chosen instruments of the protective ancestral spirits for the girl's transformation. In the space of a few swiftly passing years, Azúcar and her remarkably astute husband Lucien managed to alter the face and character of the entire *Isla*, from one side to the other; the traditional sugar production, *'la maldita caña'*, surrendered to a spectacular rise in the unimaginably profitable resort tourism industry, now focusing its lucrative operations across the entire Caribbean. Thanks in largest measure to the fearless audaciousness of vision and hope on the part of this amazing young, astute couple, the Island's fortunes increased significantly. But also unbeknownst to the ambitious couple, their protective ancestral spirits had placed both individuals in the enviable position of ushering into the ailing society an impressive number of innovative and dramatic changes with wider ramifications affecting every living soul there.

"But we must be cautious about something very essential," Marcelo was heard reminding everybody once. "Change can be quite deceptive; often no real change ever occurs, just the cleverly disguised appearance of change."

"Por todos los santos," the wise old *don* Anselmo had observed. "Maybe Lucien and his wife never fully realized the monster they created in preparing our little *Isla* for selling itself into a new kind of slavery ... far worse, maybe, than *'la maldita caña'* had ever been. The many-faced Mayanèt, in all her toughness, is always capable of dealing a surprising and very powerful blow to everybody.

"Maybe that's what this damn *sequía* is really about," Anselmo said to himself. "That sly old Mayanèt used this drought to deal us, once again, a painfully savage blow." It was true indeed. Everybody was well aware, for instance, that in the once majestic *Bosque de Flores*, for many years one of the Isla's most significant National Treasures, the *sequía* no longer allows the seductive fragrances of perfumed wild lilac and delicate jasmine, frangipani, hibiscus or jacaranda to ooze through this serene Caribbean Eden. Now, only dry, lifeless pedals serve as an ugly, faded carpet that stretches out randomly upon the no-longer meticulously manicured coral-colored flagstone walkways meandering throughout *El Bosque*. The giant bougainvillea no longer offer their natural flush of red, purple or orange leaves. The normally chatty resident monkeys no long bounce about playfully through the high tree tops. In a somewhat perverse way, the helpless, confused creatures are being robbed of their traditional habitat as they also become the unsuspecting targets of the persistent drought and Mayanèt's inexplicable vengeance. The once celestial orchids – long ago thousands of them grew beautifully inside the meticulously constructed shelters as well as outside dangling lazily under the hot tropical sun, suspended from elegant, free-standing palisades or in fairytale fashion, seemingly in mid-air with their roots without soil – are no longer the refreshing attraction in this stunning place. This once wondrous Caribbean sanctuary has now become a completely unwelcoming, morbid tomb ... all thanks to this slowly ravaging *sequía*.

"So we see," pondered the old wise one, "that Mayanèt can be sweet and protective, but at the same time showing us her tough face as she plagues us with this damn drought." For a very long time he had suspected that the sanctity of the Flower Forest was desecrated thoughtlessly by what happened there many years ago. Could it be that Mayanèt is still angry with us?

'*Bay kou bliye, pot mak sonje.*' The frequently uttered traditional Kreyòl expression means... 'Those who give out the blows forget, while those who bear the scars remember well.' Without realizing it, the community must somehow have offended Mayanèt and she never forgot.

Don Anselmo remember one very devout Catholic neighbor of his who always used to recite a particular passage from his Bible... '*The wrath of God is being revealed from Heaven against all the godless and wickedness of men who suppress the truth by their wickedness.*' Anselmo had to admit to himself that even back then, that passage made much sense. He also recalled those extremely difficult times during the early phases of the expansion project of the tourism industry on the Island. Azúcar and Lucien had played a decidedly vital role in the elaborate planning; their influential decisions impacted the lives of thousands of residents throughout the *Isla*. But matters became quite dangerous once the workers-- and most especially those poorly paid and exploited individuals laboring in the construction trades-- began realizing how they were being so mercilessly exploited. Such mistreatment had not been altogether surprising since it proved to be an easy and convenient transfer of labor practices and working conditions from the earlier, darker period of the Island's socio-economic development when sugar production singularly dominated every facet of life.

One particular gift of incalculable value from those plantation days at *Esperanza Dulce* was a young worker named Silvio Roumain. Upon becoming a member of the tourism expansion construction crew, he was soon after appointed to the strategic position of crew leader. What a crucial indication of pure destiny this appointment turned out to be. The gods were sending the workers a very clear message in the person of Silvio; there was an objective to be met... but at the time the young construction worker didn't quite realize it. When

Silvio was a little boy growing up in the *batey*, with his young, incredulous eyes, he had witnessed the ruthless, unprovoked murder of his father at the hands of the monstrous Mario Montalvo. Years later as an adept and sensible crew leader, Silvio gallantly championed unwavering solidarity among and sensible crew leader, Silvio gallantly championed unwavering solidarity among all the workers regardless of where around the Caribbean, or from whichever remote province of the *Isla* itself that that worker had come. Silvio preached in a very forceful style the traditional values of what used to be called 'coumbite,' a familiar concept that is regularly practiced even today among the populations in the Island's rural zones.

'Coumbite' goes far back in time throughout the countryside. It is the highly honored tradition of 'working together'… a vital lesson of solidarity wherein no one particular man or woman dictates orders. Instead, it is 'life itself does.' It was the charismatic and intrepid Silvio Roumain-- that precious gift from the gods – who had led the construction workers on a costly and extremely dangerous strike.

"Our collective dissent originated primarily from what we, as workers, all see as a calculated scheme of gross inequity, mistreatment, abuse and exploitation," he had said to his loyal followers. Silvio's trusted comrade since their childhood days together in the *batey*, Tomás, Jr. –having recently returned home after years engaged in rather intense indoctrination, studying and working in Revolutionary Cuba– was very instrumental in convincing Silvio to channel that boiling dissent into union organization of the workers for fighting more effectively against the widespread repression. Never before in the Island's long and tormented history had there ever been such a monumental labor movement. The strike turned into what became 'un paro general del trabajo' [a general work stoppage] that literally paralyzed labor operations throughout the *Isla*, lasting five days consecutively. The gods knew well their intent in having chosen Silvio Roumain.

TRES

Both Azúcar and Lucien had been nearly blinded by their daring, almost obsessive ambition. They remembered at a very critical moment, however, that people traditionally marginalized or left out and ignored, exploited and made to feel insignificant in the greater scheme of things, in a very short time-- and when least expected-- become the very ones who are the most dangerously resentful and on the edge. Again, there appeared a truly frightening thought to stir the anger of Mayanèt and Ezili Dantò. Even when Azúcar became convinced that tourism would be the Island's economic savior and would produce heretofore benefits and riches, the successful young entrepreneur's deepest feelings of uneasiness and nagging doubt persisted. She also began to question if she was being abandoned by her protective ancestral spirits; maybe she was even betraying their trust.

Several years later with the successful completion of her *'Pleasure Trust'* tourism project -- that's what it was ultimately named-- Azúcar confessed to *don* Anselmo alone, with great pain and reluctance, all those frightful, unsettling sentiments. She said she could not bear to disappoint Lucien, so did not share such troubling thoughts with him. Overall, news about *la sequía* was fast becoming more frightening. General alarm --but not real panic as yet-- was mounting with each news release. The drought thus far has left perhaps two million people without water and has crippled nearly half of the country's agricultural lands... at least what little there remains of it these days. The president has authorized over two billion dollars in immediate aid, but some of the rural areas hardest hit are difficult to reach. For all the lauded modernization that the country has seen, this impressive progress has benefited mainly the strategic coastal regions with an ever expanding tourism, and the border zone with its multinational assembly plants... almost immediately revealed to be 'export sweatshops' in the most brutally naked form.

And as has been customarily the case, the few major cities here on the *Isla* have been the biggest winners, especially with remarkably improved infrastructure. One government official reported that nearly seven percent of the country's croplands have been lost forever, and according to the National Weather and Climate Bureau, *"drought conditions are steadily worsening."*

"Pero coño! And so too is worsening the uncontrollable wrath of the sacred spirits," *don* Anselmo almost shouted. "As long as I can remember, we all have committed acts of shame, dishonor or remorse and therefore have greatly offended the spirits. How many times have we behaved so wickedly?"

But the old man always believed that such actions on the parts of the community were in response to a particular circumstance or situation that provoked such disgraceful behavior in the first place. "'*Todos somos culpables*' [All of us are guilty]," Anselmo used to explain to the younger farmers who were starting their plots for the first time. All farmers know that in order to grow crops, there must be trees... trees whose roots hold the precious topsoil. And naturally, this topsoil nourishes whatever is planted. Those trees will keep this rich dirt in place. The trees also will keep the cycle of rainfall going.

Doña Fela would usually add, "But there's something else all our farmers know from honored tradition and practice ... something called '*dechoukaj*'. That means that you must sometimes uproot a tree ... you simply must pull it completely out of the ground, roots and all, so that the tree will never grow back. '*Nunca jamás*' [Never again]. You do that when you are clearing a field to plant something new."

Rather sadly though, everybody remembered from that very ugly and perilous time in the *Isla* when folks automatically knew that *'dechoukaj'* described a gruesomely violent political campaign that the people collectively undertook in order to rid the society of the evil shadow of endless acts of horrendous torture, disappearances, rape, and murder of innocent citizens. *'Dechoukaj'* was applied with routine during that bloody reign of terror when, for decades, a single diabolical family had eliminated all their political opponents, dissidents and other citizens who dared challenge the *status quo*. The head of that family had been a shrewd and unscrupulous country physician who, in the most vile manner, the traditional folk religion of the people, *Vodou*. He did this simply to maintain absolute control over the entire society. Even though this family patriarch regularly admitted openly to being a *Vodou* high priest [*'palalwa'*], this fact was never substantiated historically. There was never any official documentation of his *Vodou* initiation... it was purely political theatre.

The regime routinely intimidated citizens by blatantly perpetrating unspeakable acts of violence and constantly threatening the population with 'sever harm from the sacred *lwa.*' One endless stream of despicable behaviors was used to eradicate other equally wicked behaviors. It was difficult to believe that the last heir to that feared regime– lasting fifteen years-- was allowed to return to the country after spending years of a sumptuous exile in Southern France. At the time of their hasty departure from the country, the pompous young heir and his greedy wife took with them almost the entire national treasury. The arrogant and shameless couple and their selected entourage were even escorted out of the piss-poor country on a U.S. Military aircraft... flown by an American pilot, no less. When the son returned, he was not even prosecuted for his murderous crimes against humanity'

The only official charge was that of 'corruption.' But both powerful ladies together, Mayanèt and Ezili Dantò, waited rather patiently for an inevitable vengeance. It is widely believe that now everybody, innocent and wicked alike, is paying with what they are all undergoing… this *'maldita sequía'*.

Again, don Anselmo's tone of voice revealed his sentiment. "*Carajo!* When I think about human actions of all kinds that have offended and even mocked our sacred spirits, I can never forget the terrible disgrace brought about by one operation in particular that helped pull down so many of us."

Years ago before tourism replaced *'la maldita caña'* as the main source of revenue for the *Isla*, Cristiana Montalvo, Mario's wife, for as sanctimonious as she had always pretended to be, devised a wicked scheme that exploited even more horribly the already bleeding cane workers. The bitterly unhappy elder woman seduced her long-suffering daughter-in-law Blanchette … by this time Mario's widow… to collaborate in the unprincipled scheme.

"Life would be different if you, *mi querida*, worked toward trying to alleviate other people's miseries," Cristiana had said. "Once you hear my plan to do precisely that, I'm confident that you'll agree and see matters as I do."

The two women conspired in establishing and operating with great success-- of course, carefully guarding their identities as the actual proprietors-- what they called *'la casita de placéres'* [the little house of pleasures]. They located the *'la casita'* inside the *batey*, but along a deserted stretch of land well out of view from the residents. Cristiana very shrewdly reminded … "Those wretched souls, exactly like everybody else on God's earth, nevertheless need the warmth and glow of uncomplicated human love… maybe a simple embrace, maybe even a delicate little kiss… whatever. What you and I are doing, my dear, is making it convenient for them to have that warmth even if only for a few precious hours any given night... but at a price they will be only too eager to pay."

So, what began as a single brothel soon turned into a very carefully organized and expertly operated enterprise; and indeed quite a lucrative one at that. This happened as a natural consequence of the highly profitable tourist expansion project. The initially humble '*casita de placéres*' ultimately gave way to an extremely professional escort service employing hundreds of carefully selected female and male sex workers of all ages, but most noticeably very young and vibrant, who were eager 'to service the varied needs' of international tourists now arriving in hordes daily with plenty of *pesos* to spend. Blanchette and her staunchly committed business partner, the once very pious Cristiana, managed to become closely connected with several of the Island's most fashionable all-inclusive resort complexes, especially the adults-only establishments.

Don Anselmo asked himself, "Cajaro! How was it that we just sat back on our asses and allowed that very first little whore house to get started as it did? Did we not see the unpardonable offense to our community? Were we so damn weak-minded of the flesh that we felt incapable or maybe unwilling to shut down that '*maldito negocio*' [evil business]?"

The sacred spirits couldn't help being angry and betrayed. At the time, both Fela and Mamá Lola had rebuked everybody, especially all the men of the community for seemingly not having the '*cojónes*' to burn down the despicable establishment when there was the chance to do so. Undoubtedly, the sacred spirits were disappointed with that display of cowardly behavior.

But did the gods have to wait all these many years until now for retribution? Is this what '*la maldita sequía*' is all about? Who really knows?

CUATRO

Azúcar often found herself traveling to a space back in time so long ago that she couldn't even remember how old she was at the time. She knew, though, that the place was inside the modest cabin in the *batey* with her beloved *abuelita*. It wasn't at all unusual that the journey would always include an unavoidable stop at their cabin one particularly sweltering afternoon when, as a little girl, she was allowed to leave the cane field and return alone to the cabin. It was indeed strange because no one, not even the younger children, was ever permitted to quite work earlier than scheduled. *Doña* Fela had felt uneasy about this, but said nothing ...uncharacteristic for the old woman. What happened in the *batey* that afternoon was an incident so despicable that it sent nervous ripples running through the veins of folks even remotely associated with *Esperanza Dulce*. Azúcar reflected upon the fact that her seemingly powerless neighbors knew nothing else but to accept silently and with bitter resignation the consequences of violence in whatever form. That violence against herself was to be accepted with the same muffled anger that other folks accepted regarding all the unmasked horrors of their daily circumstance then.

Time alone could never erase the memory of that terrifying afternoon for Azúcar. Her mystical saga continued unraveling over the course of many years as she made great strides during her personal and intellectual development along the path of her uncommon journey. At the same time, though, she was constantly irritated by the gargantuan efforts to find an escape from this all-too-familiar exploitation and injustice. When this amazingly intelligent young woman rose to prominence as the newly appointed regional director of a luxury tourism resort on the *Isla*, she still struggled to resist various forms of oppression and abuse. She was convinced of her own powerful and protective ancestral spirits, thanks in large part to her cherished *abuelita*. The wise and nurturing grandmother had taught her attentive young granddaughter many years earlier never to abandon her own personal *'aché '*. According to the respected elders, a person's inner power is that individual's *'aché '*; this is the special gift bestowed directly to the recipient by that person's ancestral spirit. Therefore, with this newly acknowledged inner strength, Azúcar was ultimately successful in liberating herself from her haunting demons from that distant, very ugly and cruel past. It was a difficult task to try forgetting the agonizing ordeal of self-discovery.

"Mi *querida abuelita*, my dearest grandmother," she had agonized, "I call upon you to offer me clear guidance in my personal struggles. *Querida Mayanèt*, I beg for your forgiveness and continued protection. My heart is heavy with anguish because I know that at times I have neglected you. But for the love of my soul, *'por el amor de mi alma,'* I know why there is so much turmoil churning inside me. I am sickened by what I myself unknowingly may have provoked. How blinded I was by my ambition. Believe me, I feel terribly ashamed of my selfish actions."

Everybody was rightfully proud when their little *'azúcar morenita'*, now in her new role as the competent, highly respected entrepreneur and as the bold, unyielding spokesperson for the countless individuals without a voice. She took the undisputed lead in the ongoing struggle of a wider community of exploited workers who had become entangled in the venomous web of the downside of something called *'globalization.'* It was not long after the applauses and accolades subsided that she and her husband learned in a most unfortunate manner that just below the surface of the spectacular glitter and awaiting seduction there lurked a deceptively flawed and dangerously tattered design. It was a fact that the results of the immediate success of the mammoth resort expansion project were impacting negatively the Island's entire population. The historic and vicious cycle of economic, socio-political abuse and oppression had not ceased by any measure.

Sadly, Azúcar's idyllic *Isla* had unwittingly become North America's new garment district completely outfitted with its characteristic sordidness, unbridled greed, and flagrant human rights violations and horrid working conditions. This new panorama conjured up that harsh past era of sugarcane production-- *la maldita caña*-- on the *Isla*. Whatever degree of promised rewards and benefits of modernity, the concept of globalization ushered in the presence of hideous, windowless assembly plants located behind high walls topped with sharp-edged razor wire and patrolled by heavily armed guards; these new drab-looking new facilities constituted the new *zona franca* [free trade zones]. The hordes of workers trekking in and out daily and even sometimes around the clock into these uninviting tombs were an affront to the Island's ecological dignity... and of course a total disrespect toward the ancestral spirits who prized natural splendor. The low buildings housed thousands of underpaid and oppressed workers -- undisguised tropical sweatshops. One always-watchful observer, *el viejo sabio del batey*, *don* Anselmo, reacted with a feeling of clear revulsion.

"*O zanj nan dlo*. Oh Angels in the water, why do you hide yourselves in times of trouble? We take refuge in you; save and deliver us from all this misery and evil. Keep us safe, for in you we seek refuge. How long, *O zanj*, will you hide your faces from us? How long will misery and dread triumph over us?"

Don Anselmo, along with everybody else, wanted to know what these clueless workers had done not to deserve the protection of the gods. Mamá Lola was another old soul who had pleaded to the spirits with a heavily burdened heart.

"Let us not give up hope even in this new hour of deep sadness and disappointment. We may not ever know exactly why the spirits act as they do, but we must not question their will; they have their reasons... they always do."

Another thoughtful individual, young Silvio, had remarked to an assembled crowd at the time of the general strike.

"*Kochón-yo Kotan; men, moun-yo pa kontan*," meaning, 'the pigs are happy; but the people are not.' Everything comes with a price and Ii just hope we all are prepared and willing to pay that price."

Lucien Saint Jacques had spoken for the influential international consortium of powerful overseas interests when he remarked some years ago immediately before the collapse of the corrupt government at the time. "Multinationals are solidly convinced of one thing regarding the president of a small country like ours. For instance, when that president exhibits selfish desires of continuity in office in the midst of significant tourism expansion and designs for massive deportations of undocumented workers living in the country, he will most certainly fail. His government cannot and will not be able to harmonize an effective re-election campaign with pending structural adjustment policies. His plans are not only egotistical and foolish, but also are grossly counterproductive."

"*Cela fait partie de la comédie.*" [It's all part of the game]. That was the assessment of Azúcar's best friend and long-time confidant, the writer Marie Chauvet. "How absolutely correct Lucien was in his astute observation."

Not too long following Lucien's somber prediction, the president was indeed forced to step down; almost immediately he was convicted of fraud and embezzlement involving one of the Island's largest banks. The disgraced president was granted exile in an exclusive, gated enclave in Southern Florida, where there also resided with a certain understood anonymity numerous other former high ranking political and military figures from various parts of Latin American and the Caribbean.

"*Peyi-a ap fini nam lanmé*"…'The country is going to end up in the sea.' *Don* Anselmo's prophetic remark would be heard again and again. Azúcar found herself standing rather solemnly, perhaps transfixed, at the expansive window of her always safe and comfortable family room at *La Morenita* Estate. She was looking out upon an unbroken panorama of the estate's landscape: nearly barren trees, scrubs, and bushes. What to her always had been a plethora of lush and enviable sumptuousness-- a pure delight to the human eye as well as to the olfactory senses-- was now something altogether unrecognizable. Looking out the window, she was witnessing Nature's cruel and unjustifiable punishment. The otherwise resplendent view was under a senselessly vicious attack by blight, drabness, and deprivation in every direction.

"Goddamn it! *La maldita sequía,*" she cursed. She didn't even realize that she was sobbing... quietly at first, then loudly as she began feeling the better sting of another kind of grief. Lucien, the single passionate love of her entire life, was now deceased. The abandonment she felt that resulted from the death of her *abuelita* had left a definite spiritual emptiness in her heart for many years afterwards... perhaps without ever being filled. The intensity of these two deaths, she had decided, could not possibly be measured in terms of proportion; she loved deeply both these two very powerful and special human beings. So, she wept; but she also wept for the ugliness that she saw outside with almost equal grief.

At that moment, Alegra entered the room where her mother was still gazing out the window. The young woman had heard the loud crying escaping from the room; she was worried about her mother, thinking mistakenly of course, that the grief of long departed loved one had run its course. After all, many years had passed since the loss of her father and of her great-grandmother *doña* Fela. Alegra had been diligently pursuing a post-graduate fellowship in climate science and world geological studies at the University of Toronto, her father's *alma mater*, when she received that most distressing long-distance telephone call; Lucien had suffered a fatal heart attack. She interrupted her studies and rushed immediately back to the *Isla* so that she could be at her mother's side, offering much needed and well appreciated emotional support. Alegra secretly agonized about the real possibility of her mother's complete mental collapse. The weight of Lucien's sudden death exacted a noticeable psychological toll from the grieving widow.

Still at the window, mother and daughter embraced each other tenderly as they each began nostalgically recalling earlier days of shared joy and wonder. Lucien had built the breathtakingly beautiful and spacious *La Morenita* for his new bride. Azúcar caught herself giggling in girlish fashion when she reflected with maternal delight upon an inherently bright and inquisitive eight-year old little *'princesa.'*

She asked her daughter, *"Mi querida Alegrita,* do you remember how every morning after your father finished his breakfast and left for work, you would feed your adorable little pets-- that playful family of vervet monkeys?"

"Ay dios mío, mami; you actually remember that?" she replied as she too giggled almost uncontrollably like a young school girl.

"Pues, claro que sí, hi hijita. [Well, of course, my dear child.] You told your father and me that you came upon the idea to feed the monkeys so as to prevent the frisky little creatures from stealing all the ripe, low-hanging mangoes and *guayabas* from the trees that shaded the veranda."

They both chuckled loudly as they stood together in loving embrace. The mother recalled the episode as though it had happened only last week; the daughter thought about how the idea itself of routinely feeding those little animals was admittedly quite creative for an eight-year old. Lucien, upon hearing what his little *princesa* had done, was extremely proud of Alegrita's keen sensitivity and keen intellect as indicated by the child's actions.

"Our *princesita* possesses truly problem-solving skills at such a young age," said the doting father. Thereafter, Lucien aggressively, but carefully, nurtured and encouraged the continuous intellectual development of the tender young scholar.

CINCO

"*Lafanmi se lavi* [The Family is Life]," Azúcar's grandmother would readily have said, as Azúcar herself now did, turning aside from joyous reflections of Alegra's childhood. The mother was recalling those undeniably precious moments watching her little *princesa* develop so wonderfully in every regard. Azúcar once again focused on what both mother and daughter saw presently from the window in the family room. In what could only be described as a wide-eyed gaze, they became saddened by what they saw.

"*Mi hiita*," Azúcar confessed to her daughter, "Forgive me for what I'm about to say. But deep inside my heart I am spared the additional plain of knowing how hurt your dear father would be if he were here right now with us to witness this horrible destruction caused by this *sequía*. I won't pretend to understand any of this."

She then closed her aggrieved eyes and silently wished that her *abuelita* were indeed present with her in this moment to help explain why the sacred spirits all seemed to be responding in this particular manner to any number of disapproving actions on the part of the Island's residents. Azúcar found it all quite puzzling.

"*Por todos los santos, ayúdame entender.*" [For the sake of all the saints, help me understand.] It troubled her that she did not say this aloud to her young scientist daughter; she wanted to do so, but did not. For Azúcar, one regrettable fact was that Alegra, at this important stage in her scholarly pursuits, was unlike her mother, even though both of them were university-strained. After all, mother, like daughter, had also left the *Isla* in order to gain a more contemporary world view. Alegra, thoroughly scientifically-minded, very purposely distanced herself from what her community had long regarded as an automatic adherence to traditional beliefs and practices... most of which were still deeply entrenched in the thinking and actions of residents in every section of the *Isla*.

Without question, *doña* Fela, as well as other *'viejos sabios del batey'* like Mamá Lola and *don* Anselmo, would be disappointed and even hurt as a result of the young scholar's outright rejection of honored traditions. As a young child, Alegra had been tutored rigorously by a carefully selected individual who was extremely well versed in all aspects of the community's traditional culture and values. These values played a vital role in her mother's life. Alegra had been awarded a prestigious academic scholarship to study geology and climate science at the University of Colorado. Upon completing her second year of undergraduate studies, she again received a notable honor. She was recognized for her outstanding scholarship that resulted in her being selected to join a team of other gifted young geologists and climatologists, along with a few senior professors, on an expedition that would take the team of investigators on a journey to several world sites that had been experiencing critical drought conditions over a period of time.

The team traveled to the African continent, for instance, in order to study firsthand the desertification in the Sahel region-- a 3,000-mile wide belt in Western Africa situated immediately south of the Sahara Desert. In this region, 19 million people are living on the edge of malnutrition due mainly to severe drought conditions. Alegra was astonished by what she learned about this unusual transition zone between the massive desert situated to the north of the wetter zones of equatorial Africa to the south. However, this impressive swath of sub-Sahara savanna faces a crisis on two fronts: one of a political nature, the other, humanitarian concerns. She also spent a brief period in the turbulent country of Somalia, observing remarkable geological formations.

"What we are experiencing currently here on our own *Isla* is duplicating a distinct pattern that we've seen throughout history-- most specifically with the ancient Mayan civilization of Southern Mexico and the region of Central America," Alegra began to explain, not at all in a strictly professional tone, but much more in a kind of very engaging, matter-of-fact manner... "Scientists can now present us with conclusive empirical evidence that the collapse of the that glorious Mayan culture was likely due to a relatively mild *sequía*, much like the drier conditions expected in the coming years in places like the Sahel; all this is due to climate change, without question."

Researchers have now reported that their analysis shows that the smaller amounts of rain meant that open water sources in pools and lakes evaporated faster than could be replaced by more precipitation.

Alegra continued by stating, "The data further suggest that the main cause was an amazing decrease in summer storm activity; summer, of course, was the main season for cultivation and replenishment of Mayan fresh water systems."

As is evidenced, there are no rivers in the Yucatan lowlands. Therefore, one can readily see in today's Sahel, for instance, societal disruptions and abandonment of cities are very much the consequences of critical water shortages, mainly because there seems to have been a rapid, repetition of multi-year droughts. International climate experts have predicted that in certain regions of the world, similar dry spells-- *sequías*-- are most probably on the way due to climate change. While modern societies like those in the Caribbean, to a certain degree, are expected to be much better equipped to handle drought, there are many risks that still remain. In regions like the Sahel, the risks are monumental, as Alegra's investigative team saw while there. What seems like a minor reduction in water availability may well lead to important, long-lasting problems. This situation is not all unique to the Yucatan Peninsula, the epicenter of the ancient Mayan culture, but applies to all those regions in similar settings where evaporation is high. Such is the case with Alegra's small Caribbean *Isla.*

"But we don't have to go that far to see what's happening regarding climate change," the observant young scientist was quick to add. "Just look at the case of the United States. A sharp rise in food prices there, for instance, has grown steadily after long- standing drought prompted the federal government to actually declare a natural disaster in large sections of the U.S. Midwest. Conditions in the four main wheat-producing states, Kansas, Oklahoma, Texas, and where I went to university– in Colorado-- continue being the worst on the record. *La sequía* in that region has carried over from what nearly everybody experienced as the hottest year on record in the United States."

Alegra finished what her mother considered a scholarly dissertation, as she would later boast to friends. The mother expressed the same exuberance with Alegra's keen grasp of such lofty concepts as she had when the little *princesa* was a precocious eight-year old and had resolved the predicament of her pet monkeys and the stolen fruit from the trees shading the veranda. However, the proud mother didn't dare admit even to herself how painfully wounded her grandmother would be because of Alegra's personal decision to ignore totally *'the much stronger powers'* of the sacred island spirits.

Once becoming intoxicated by *'the powers of science and reason'*, Alegra alienated herself farther and farther from what she and some of her more smug university classmates regarded as *'foolish superstitions and foundless myths.'* Old *Doña* Fela would very sadly have wondered,

"*Por todos los santos,* this what a fool's education does to a person?"

Don Anselmo and Mamá Lola would likewise be greatly disheartened by Alegra's daring rejection of all that was considered sacred; Alegra, it was later revealed, had become an atheist. Even her dear *'madrina'* [godmother], Marie Chauvet, her mother's closest friend and acclaimed writer of contemporary issues and various aspects of Caribbean culture, was unable to come to grips with her goddaughter's radical conversion to something so distinctly alien from the vital core of traditional Caribbean thinking. Initially, Azúcar felt a deep concern about Alegra's apparently defiant choice-- especially at so early a stage in her development as an independent and intelligent college co-ed-- regarding her personal religious or spiritual convictions. But later, she resigned herself just by accepting the hard reality that her brilliant young *princesa* was much like her father Lucien in this regard.

Both she and her father were void of the effects of full immersion into the complexities of the often strikingly unconventional religious life of the old *batey* community. It was clear that Alegra soon forgot [or perhaps consciously *erased*?] all the lessons that her beloved nanny Virgile had so responsibly imparted during so many afternoon tutoring sessions years ago. An intense love and devotion to modern science, along with the rapid advancement in technology, had completely filled up Alegra's new space that was eager for intellectual challenge and nourishment. Her mother remained silent, incapable of doing anything else.

Virgile would most certainly be in disbelief at the young scholar's unexpected, but exciting transformation. Alegra's steadfast dedication to science would surely mystify Virgile. It was Mamá Lola, though, who had insisted forcefully that both Lucien and Azúcar hire this special individual because of her clearly unapologetic and ardent fostering of local traditions and unique religious concepts.

"Better that one of our own trusted community elders... someone like Virgile, serve as *'maestra'* [teacher] for our *princesa;* only then would our little *princesa* definitely earn the truest values of the ancestors," Mamá Lola had affirmed when this particular nanny was hired.

"Such precious values," everyone felt, "could not possibly be taught by somebody contracted through some fancy agency located in faraway Toronto."

Strenuous disapproval, of course, would have come from these cultural purists, unwavering in their strict obedience to the scared ancestral spirits. For the most part, these purists believed that... "every circumstance in life, every behavior or activity associated with our daily life, every thought... absolutely everything is a direct result of the gods, with rewards and punishments given out according to our obedience or disobedience to undisputed will of the gods." It had been Virgile who taught the child the ancient creed that, in those days, all children learned even before they learned the alphabet. "*I believe in Bondye, the Almighty Father of the sky, who manifests his spiritual nature in me; in a large number of spirits; and in all things visible and invisible.*"

So then, there was no allowance for even the slightest degree of intrusion or dominance by something called 'scientific inquiry.'

Virgile routinely ended her tutorial sessions with telling her pupil, "*Pa bliye sa ma di̧ w. Dio kler va koule devan ou.* [Don't forget what I'm telling you. Clear water will now flow in front of you.]" What awaited everyone who dearly loved Alegra would be a shockingly new truth.

SEIS

Unfortunately, however, the clear water that poor Virgile warned little Alegra about was not destined to flow in front of the innocent *princesa* ... at least not for some time yet to come. Alegra soon forgot all those perceived urgent afternoon cultural tutorials that Virgil had so eagerly provided her young mentee. There were all those treasured beliefs and practices, those sometimes puzzling traditional Kreyòl sayings and delicious slices of ancient wisdom-- passed down from one generation to the next, all those undeniably playful, but initially difficult-to-decipher *Cric? Crak!* riddles, all those odd-sounding, but fun-to-pronounce names in the seemingly endless pantheon of ancestral deities: Danbala, Ezili Dantó, Changó, Gede, Mayanét, Obatalá, Ogou, Papá Legba, Gran Ti-Jean Petwo; all those colorful, rhythmic festivals and ceremonies --some of them rather solemn, others quite jubilant.

Of course there were always those popular children's games, even many of the culture's most succulent traditional meals, also the deeper meanings of the various spectacular *'drapo'* [flag] usually on prominent display along the walls of the large and impressive *'ounfò'* [ceremonial temple] located in the forest clearing a short walking distance from *La Morenita*. So many important aspects of the Island's traditional culture, shared among the *batey* community since the very early days of Alegra's great-grandmother *doña* Fela and very carefully passed down to successive generations by the respected elders like *don* Anselmo and Mamá Lola and others, were regularly positioned alongside the more formal and dutifully learned Catholic traditions.

"Por todos los santos de mi alma", the elders always used to remind everybody, thrusting upward to the skies one clinched

fist. "Where one something stands firm, something else stands beside it."

At this, the elder then raised the other clinched fist to illustrate the point. He once said, "These wonderfully coordinated and intertwining traditions will most surely provide our little *princesa* with the kind of armored fortification of confidence and strength she will need later in the challenging outside world that she is about to enter."

Both parents agreed; they were therefore justifiably proud of what they very thoughtfully had planned for their child.

"No doubt about it; our Alegrita is equipped with a wholesome balance of Island reality and excellent survival strategies that will protect her," her father Lucien observed, ignoring altogether the ancient and sacred Island spirits. Azúcar's and Lucien's sense of accomplishment was solidly conclusive when their little scholar, because of her consistent hard work and diligence, won, first, an undergraduate scholarship and later a fellowship to pursue graduate studies in the United States. But what for many earlier years had been a matter of routine indoctrination, repetition, and memorization turned into well concealed, personal tedium and meaningless chatter-- many times just nonsense -- for the young pupil. Competing rigorously and standing increasingly firmer beside all the widely revered Island lore and mystic cosmology was Alegra's fierce thirst for the study of geology... 'the scientific study of the origin, history, and structure of the earth and of specific region of the earth's crust.' The burning issues of climate phenomena also intrigued her. These interests, daunting as they were, completely overwhelmed and easily diminished every single aspect of the intense instruction for which Virgile was responsible on a daily basis over the years. Alegra was in her final year of secondary school-- almost ready to depart *la Isla* for undergraduate studies when the unexpected happened. Nearly everybody was caught off guard.

"*Mi querida Virgile*. My dear Virgile," the otherwise attentive Alegra began rather sheepishly as she addressed her respected mentor one afternoon well before their tutorial session had even started.

"I have a confession to make. And truly, Virgile, I don't mean to hurt you in the least nor cause your kind and gentle heart to be in pain. For my mother's sake, that's the very last thing I'd want to do. The fact is that I myself am in pain to have to tell you this."

Virgile was startled; she said nothing, but continued listening to a nervous, reluctant young pupil whom the woman did not recognize.

"I must admit to you in honesty that I see no true purpose in all this. All these lessons every day. I know that *mami* and *papi* both want me to learn everything that you've been teaching me, but I just don't feel it... I'm not getting anything from all this confusing stuff."

Virgile was visibly numb for speech; her wide mouth opened even wider than seemed possible for a human; her deeply wrinkled, usually steady, strong jaws dropped suddenly and appeared to become locked into place. In an instant, flashing rapidly before the old woman's still disbelieving eyes were stark images of her honored comrades *doña* Fela, *don* Anselmo, and Mamá Lola and several other recognizable faces from the faded memories of the old *batey* at *Esperzanza Dulce*. She saw clearly the dispirited faces of young Silvio, of Tomás, Jr., of one-eyed Clementina and her husband Tomás, Sr.; also of Lolita and her '*beautiful Haitian Estimé*' [as she alone used to refer to her husband; long-neck Teresa and her very prankster-loving husband Cirilo, and of course there appeared the face of 'naughty-by-nature', big-bosomed Sarafina, who scandously ended up serving as the live-in concubine to the old and crippled plantation '*capataz*', the irascible *don* Diego Montalvo.

It was immediately after the rapid flash of the faces of these ghosts from the past that the old woman released an audible shriek of horror and disbelief, refusing stubbornly to accept what her old, but still quite sharp ears had just heard dripping from the tender lips of the youngster seated in front of her.

"*Que mi Bondye me libra de todo lo malo; qué estás diciéndome?*" [May my good Lord deliver me from all evil; what are you telling me?]. Virgile directed her remarks to Alegra with controlled alarm, not anger. The old woman expressed dismay; with absolute firmness, however, she was anxious to have answers to a host of tortuous questions.

"*Pero cómo es posible?*" But how is this possible? What will your mother say to all this? How will you ever know who you are or know your connection to your past... or who you are today?" These were troubling questions, indeed. With unmasked disappointment and sadness, the elderly mentor and human repository of the *Isla's* most cherished spiritual treasures and sacred traditions now expressed her deep lament at the raw sentiment on the part of her young pupil who was about to leave for her anxiously awaited university studies.

"*Mi h'jita,* [My sweet child], you perhaps don't realize how much you have betrayed your *aché* ... your own personal protective spirit. Sometimes in order to see the light, you must risk the darkness. *Naje pou w soti*; that's an old traditional Kreyòl saying that means 'Swim to get out.'"

Having now gained a more emboldened confidence, Alegra attempted to explain to a visibly wounded Virgile all those repressed feelings over so many years of the old woman's well informed and thoughtful instruction, all those many daily lessons.

Alegra was genuine in her offered apology. "*Perdóname, Tata.* Please forgive me, Auntie Virgile. But as I tried so many times to confess to you -- with all my heart--that I just don't feel anything about all that you've taught me; I never really did. There was just so much information. Honestly, *Tata,* these teachings are so very beautiful in so many ways; everything you taught me was so totally new. And there's no question that

I could never have learned such things in school. But honestly, Virgile, all of that for me is so out-of-touch with modern concepts of science and technology... which has become the true focus of my desire to learn all about the real world. For a long time before he died, my *papi* always knew exactly how much the study of geology and climate meant to me. He knew that this has always been my passion, and I'm not ashamed to admit openly that modern science blocks out all the confusion about protective gods or my personal *aché*."

Virgile continued listening with her characteristic patience, but in unaltered shock and discomfort. "*O zanj nan dlo* [Oh Angels in the water]," she said, now addressing those sacred spirits '*nan dlo*' as she petitioned them for the their understanding and compassion for Alegra's misguided sentiment, not reprisal or retribution. Above all else, Virgile wished for illumination and reason in her young pupil's case.

"*Por el amor de todo lo sagrado.* [For the sake of everything sacred], this poor soul must not be forsaken-- even though without knowing it she has betrayed her own *aché*. Clear water surely did not flow in front of this innocent child. The sacred spirits all know how hard I myself tried to carry out my duties in providing this sweet child with those important things she needed to know about. Did I somehow fail in my efforts? Did I somehow not do what was expected of me? How was it possible? I know about our most honored traditions and beliefs. Why did this happen? The sacred spirits must allow this child to 'swim out of this'...

'*Naje pou w soti*'."

It was Alegra's turn to respond to her mentor's despondency. "I suspect that *mami* will be terribly disappointed with me; I know that if *abuelita* Fela were still alive, she too would be disappointed. So would *papi*. But believe me, dear Virgile, it's not at all your fault. You did everything that was expected of you. I'm sure *mami* will realize this. Please don't blame yourself for my lack of interest. *Tata*, it's not that I disrespect you; you know that I would never do such a thing. I just feel that the old traditions of our *Isla* are so antiquated and have no meaningful place in my world today-- a modern world of solid scientific inquiry and inquiry. To me, everything else is just superstition, and I say this without ever meaning to insult you or all the other truly good and beautiful people here on the *Isla*. But, Virgile that's all this is to me... superstition. But this is still the only home I know and always will be."

The old nanny bristled upon hearing that fully charged and singularly offensive word *'superstition'*. Her skin grew cold. All her life, she, along with everybody else in the *batey*, had suffered the gross indignities and insults leveled by most 'outsiders' and 'non-believers' whenever these individuals used the descriptive labels 'superstitious' and even 'devil worshipers.' But on this particular occasion, Virgile chose not to respond; she genuinely could not react to this latest affront coming from someone so young and innocent and coming from affront coming from someone so young and innocent and coming from the mouth of someone whom the old woman loved so deeply. It was always as though little Alegrita were her own child; even though in her lifetime Virgile had had three or maybe four serious *'amantes'*[paramours], none of those relationships ever produced a single child because Virgile could not conceive; only a few of her closest friends in the *batey* knew this.

"I remember when I was much younger how I used to watch how *mami* allowed herself to become wrapped up in *abuela* Fela's very narrow, antiquated way of looking at things and then would decide how to act according to which way the little cowrie shells scattered on the ground once they were thrown down. Really weird, I thought to myself. I'll never forget how *mami* always insisted upon taking me into the altar room with her. Well, the honest truth is that I just couldn't accept her way of looking at life, even at that young age. Cowrie shells scattered on the ground that could reveal a person's destiny? Altar rooms? Scared *'drapo'* hanging along the walls? *Baka* [little demons]? *Gwim wa* [wizard manuals]? Really, Virgile, when it comes to what I want for my own future, it certainly doesn't involve sitting on the floor of the local *ounfò* watching people swirl around as though they were in some kind of trance or maybe tipsy from drinking a too much *'clarin'* [raw sugarcane rum]."

Another horrible offense gushed from the young scholar, although totally unintended, but nevertheless launching a further stinging blow to the delicate sensitivity of the already wounded tutor. Virgile, however, remained stoic in her disposition and still said nothing. She realized with great remorse how Alegra was thoroughly *'out of touch and ignorant'*– in Virgile's words– Alegra was concerning the realities, spiritual and otherwise, of their beautiful little *Isla*. It was a place heavily infused with the sacred traditions and often complex beliefs profoundly revered by most folk who have remained faithful and obedient over centuries. How sad, indeed, that 'clear water did not flow in front' of the scholarly Alegra. Much in the pattern of her talented mother at the same age, the young Alegra excelled in all her academic studies and consistently displayed an eager inquisitiveness about everything. Without the slightest degree of envy, all her classmates genuinely admired Alegra and actually found her fascinating-- perhaps mainly because she came from the 'exotic tropics,' as her classmates often said of Alegra's place of origin. Alegra was secretly embarrassed by what she found as a narrowly limited knowledge of geography on the part of these classmates; many of them didn't know the difference between one Caribbean island and another... with the possible exception of maybe Cuba and Jamaica. But all in all, her closest friends considered her a 'true genius.'

Alegra's impressively keen interest and penchant for exploration and discovery readily seized the attention of all her professors at the university; with unrestrained unanimity they felt that the young Caribbean scholar would be duly rewarded with a splendid career in the related fields of geology and climatology. In fact, a few senior professors in the university community had determined quite early that Alegra could be positioned among their most promising science students and as such should be rigorously challenged and closely monitored by their watchful and endearing eyes. Definite plans, they decided, lay ahead for Alegra.

"Most assuredly, rarely have I had the sheer pleasure of teaching a pupil so thoroughly focused and so authentically excited by the wonders of the physical universe," remarked one of Alegra's professors.

"Indeed so," readily agreeing a department colleague. "And I especially find it absolutely refreshing to have a *female* student so absorbed in scientific research and inquiry." His stunning remarks were, of course, quite condescending and gender biased; was he even aware of his horribly offensive observation?

"Extremely surprising and also impressive," said the first professor. "I understand that she comes to us with a rather impressive academic preparation."

"Did you know that her parents were respected members of the Island's influential financial sector and also socially progressive? Her mother is a former Speaker of the Island's Congress and a very successful entrepreneur. Her now father, now deceased, was Lucien Saint Jacques, a very prominent Canadian financial strategist and corporate attorney with one of Canada's most powerful multinational investment capital firms. I hear the family is one of the richest in the entire Caribbean."

Then the other professor injected a revealing personal observation. "Thank God for the fact that the girl hasn't come with a trunk full of Caribbean black magic potions and all that other terrifying Voodoo mumbo-jumbo stuff. Truly, that shit would clearly obstruct any degree of meaning in an otherwise challenging pursuit of modern scientific investigation. "He and his colleague both laughed triumphantly at this observation.

"You're absolutely right. You know, of course, that the majority of those people down there are thoroughly wrapped up in their ridiculous superstitions that have hindered any serious progress for decades. I'm just thrilled to see that our young Alegra, with so much exciting potential, wasn't fallen victim like so many others. It's sad that most of them are so blinded by muddy water." Both doting professors beamed smugly and breathed what they felt was a well-deserved relief. They agreed that Alegra brought a fresh new spirit to the classroom and were proud to consider themselves 'very enlightened educators' … "We're truly blessed to have this receptive young mind in our midst."

"*Dlo ker va koule devan ou,*" whispered a soft voice from somewhere far out of earshot from this 'enlightenment.'

SIETE

"Environmental stress due to severe rain deficit." How absurd! It's almost laughable if the situation itself were not so dire." That's how the media throughout the *Isa* decided to describe advancing drought crisis... calling it *'environmental stress.'* Chelaine didn't bother to finish reading the morning paper as she customarily did every morning while having breakfast. Having once been an award-winning photo-journalist and conscientious newspaper columnist for many years, she was naturally angered by what she saw as 'media deception' or outright avoidance altogether by those entities supposedly responsible for *'la pura verdad'* [the pure truth]. She crumbled the newspaper and tossed it violently onto the flagstone floor of the veranda where she had been sitting since breakfast.

"Por mi santa madre. Silvio would be outraged," she yelled in her own anger. "The bastards play at honest journalism, never having the *'cojones'* to tell their readers the truth about the world's food crisis, for instance." Official United Nations reported that one billion people are already going hungry and another two billion will be affected by the year 2050. It was clearly a crisis that was worsening as more intensive heat waves reverse the rising crop yields.

Chelaine knew all too well that overwhelming new research indicates that severe heat waves currently in Australia are expected to become many times more likely in coming decades due to global warming. The extreme heat led to the year 2012 becoming the hottest year recorded in the United States, for instance. "They don't even use the word *'sequía'*; plain and simple, it's a damn drought!"

With a mixture of sadness and rage, sitting on her veranda still, Chelaine witnessed how all the flowering vegetation was now just a massive blanket of dull brown and shriveled from an obvious neglect of desperately needed moisture. The normally hardy ferns had lost all their usually crisp freshness; the *flamboyán*, as well as all the bougainvilleas, were absent of even the mere suggestion of blossoms. And as perhaps the conclusive assault upon Chelaine's senses, the early morning breezes that always used to drift lazily of the turquoise ocean no longer carried the alluring fragrances of jasmine and lavender. Missing also were the delicious aromas of the *Isla's* world renown, mammoth collection of glorious orchids, housed safely in *'El Bosque de Flores,'* The Flower Forest. Since as long as she and everyone else could remember, at this time during the day and again during the period between sunset and darkness, anyone standing outside almost anywhere on the *Isla* was favored with the most rare of Nature's gifts... the delicate concoction of diverse aromas drifting from the depths of *El Bosque*. However, now no such emissions were possible because of the *maldita sequía*.

Chelaine was overcome by nausea; the current reality was just that powerful. She began thinking about her deceased husband Silvio, who perhaps more than any other human being, always found himself in perfect harmony with Nature; he genuinely respected and admired the simplest of Nature's elements. Silvio, as she reminisced now, never considered minimally insignificant the various dimensions of Nature. Many years ago when Chelaine first described to her mother the exciting and dynamic young man she had met, the feisty young woman was very clear in identifying the man she would later marry.

"I've never met a more extraordinary, more intelligent, talented and socially conscious individual before now. He possesses such an abundance of humanity; he is so sufficiently handsome as to reward the full attention of any of my potential rivals who might be pursuing him without it being necessary in the slightest to drag into question his pedigree, his university title, if any, or his lineage. The only thing that is important and relevant to me is that I love him so very deeply. I trust completely in my love for Silvio Roumain with the same intensity of faith and passion that he does in me."

Silvio had said to his brothers Toussaint and Jérôme at the time when describing his future wife, "She is now my new hope and single consolation. I have never known another woman as sharply intelligent and alert as Chelaine."

The young woman's mother, Blanchette Montalvo Origène Desgraves, very strangely, had remained chillingly silent with this unexpected and discomforting disclosure from her daughter. Blanchette's mind retraced with deliberate slowness the painful steps taken in the process of reaching the point of her current time, space, and particular circumstance. The older woman had been left a widow; her husband Mario was murdered in grotesque fashion after having led a life of wickedness and cruelty with impunity-- especially toward the countless defenseless sugarcane workers at *Esperanza Dulce*. In that moment of her daughter's earnest confession of love for the handsome sugarcane cutter, Blanchette thought about Mario's selfish and devastating abandonment of his wife and their twin baby girls Chelaine and Cécile.

"I've learned many things as I've grown older… particularly after your father died as he did. None of us were prepared for his sudden death… a total shock it was. But there's absolutely no doubt in my mind that the most important lesson I learned about life is that every single human being, regardless of their status or the circumstance in which they find themselves … that person needs and deserves the maximum warmth and glow of unconditional love… in whatever corner they find it and for however long it is available to them."

Of course, though, Blanchette never dared mention to anyone, and least not to her twin girls --even when they became sophisticated, world-traveled adult women-- that it had been she and her unscrupulous mother-in-law Cristiana Montalvo, the pristine, very Catholic wife of the evil *'capataz'* at *Esperanza Dulce, don* Diego Montalvo, who together had devised the clandestine and distasteful scheme of exploiting the open weaknesses of the already miserable souls in the *batey.*

"We are merely selling love, *mi querida...* if only for an hour at a time," as Cristiana had said in order to convince her woefully naïve daughter-in-law when they set up the sinister operation for the eager cane workers.

Silvio Roumain was that same very courageous and charismatic individual, as everybody felt, whom the sacred, unifying spirits Mayanèt and Ezili Dantò had deliberately chosen to intervene in the lengthy and arduous struggle of the workers in the construction trades to form a union. To have an effective union was always the supreme goal in the general welfare of the Island's oppressed work force. Silvio and Chelaine were extremely pleased with the triumphant mission since all government regimes as far back as anyone could recall had fiercely banned union organization and union activity in any form. Additionally, there had been the agonizing, often forgotten plight of the *Isla's 'zona franca'* [free trade zone] assembly plants, mainly the textile and garment industry sweatshops. An enormous new free trade zone was created in a town on the other side of the border, Ouanaminthe, for the purpose of attracting international assembly and operations of various kinds for export. The scheme was simple: employ cheap labor. Initially, workers -- for the most part innocent, underage girls and young women desperate for work-- were to be paid US$1.74 daily, which was shamefully well below the internationally-set poverty line of US$2.00 per day.

"The ongoing growth of low-wage production in the export-processing zones of our *Isla* can only be described as part of a larger, more aggressive and evil scheme for bringing total industrialization of the whole country... meaning, of course, a parallel, even more brutal exploitation of workers," Silvio had articulated forcefully.

Chelaine's intensive investigation into the new Ouanaminthe *zona franca*, now the country's largest facility, revealed the disgusting sordidness, the inhumane working conditions, and the overall abuse of thousands of workers.

"*Se on ki pou mété lod lan sa!*" [We are the ones who will straighten things out!] *Don* Anselmo had uttered a familiar response in his sense of revolt. He had experienced more than his share of being tested over the years of his long life. Terrifying eye-witness accounts from many young women who worked at the monstrous complex had easily solidified the old man's revulsions. "Some really horrible things happening over there," he added, nearly making him want to vomit.

As Chelaine closed her eyes-- after painfully continuing to look out from the veranda at the deteriorating vegetation-- she remembered Silvio's final battle to "*make things right*," as he had put it. Her stalwart champion had determined, if it meant sacrificing his very life, to bring a decisive end to the abuses too long endured by sweatshop workers. The inevitable did happen. He, together with a few other dedicated co-conspirators in the struggle, died in a in a ghastly vehicle crash while *en route* to Ouanaminthe, transporting a truckload of powerful explosives. The objective of the carefully conceived plan was to blow up the giant facility. Silvio had always emphasized to his wife and their young son Estimé that…"*the place closest to the Divine is love itself and that becoming intoxicated by the sweetness of life is the vital centerpiece of existence.*"

The assembly workers throughout the Island network of free trade zone plants eventually won the legal right to unionize; they also won safer workplace conditions, in addition to securing a pay rate of almost double the minimum wage for a revolutionary new six-day week. It was unbelievable. When Chelaine finally opened her eyes, she realized the total impact of the drought that was slowly encroaching upon her weakened sensibilities, particularly now that she no longer could count on her heroic warrior being at her side to bolster her. Jointly, her reflections served to reinforce for her *"the sanctity of live"* that her gallant warrior had so often spoken about. Tragically, though, she saw everything around her gradually withering away. The subtle process was not at all unlike the low-hovering bougainvillea in the garden or the large clumps of Antillean hydrangea gracefully encircling the entire house.

As a distraught Chelaine reflected upon her deceased Silvio and about how he surely would react to what was now visible in every direction; she also turned her thoughts towards her twin sister Cécile.

"My dear sister has always been in such perfect synchronization with her politically conscious husband Tomás, Jr., and I haven't the slightest doubt that they both wouldn't also see this present climate dilemma as further and very strong evidence of the very negative and damaging consequences of abusive corporate capitalism."

Of course, it was true. Cécile and Tomás, Jr. shared the same embedded ideological formation as a result of living and working in Cuba. "That revolutionary society changed so many aspects of both our lives-- but mine especially," Cécile had said, "that our love for each other and the way we learned to view the world offered us an inner peace plus an overwhelming serenity that we perhaps could never have found anywhere else, but most definitely not here in our own *Isla*."

Her husband had made a quite strident observation at that time. "It's completely true that people here are finally beginning to admit to themselves-- as painful as the truth can often be-- the conscious reality of their miserable circumstance. For such a long time, our people were trapped in the psychological *batey* of this Island's reality. *Coño!* The whole goddamn Island was becoming one gigantic and deceptive *batey*."

Cécile and her husband eventually became naturalized citizens of their adopted Cuban society. They had known that for centuries their own Island's economic and socio-political core had been *la maldita caña de azúcar* [the cursed sugarcane]. Every component of life revolved without disruption around a deliberately crafted and closely monitored system; it was a system that proved lucrative far beyond imagination. The legendary *cañaverales* [sugarcane fields]-- lush and green, and seemingly innocent-- could be sighted from all directions, stretching to the horizon. The system first utilized forced slave labor before later implementing a nefarious scheme of bringing in contract laborers that had been recruited from nearby islands where high unemployment was chronic. The recruits found themselves positioned only slightly above the level of previous plantation slavery and easily numbered in the hundreds on large family-owned sugar estates. During the period when multinational corporations purchased these profitable estates, the grinding capacity reached from 20,000 to 30,000 short tons of sugar per day. *Azúcar* was undisputed 'King' of the Island's revenue producer.

There were still acceptable sugar harvest yields during the initial development of the tourism industry and the rise of the interrelated construction trades. Profit margins for sugar production were noticeably impressive considering the circumstances of a fast-growing tourism in the region. But now, the unbelievable sight of withering twelve-to-fifteen-foot cane stalks, and the completely missing exotic flowering bloom-- sometimes white, sometimes pink-- that was always perched at the tip of each stalk standing row upon row like sentinels, offered a real challenge to the eye. Entire fields were dressed in a revolting shades of brown that was even uglier than cow dung. Cécile was sickened by what she was now witnessing.

"Anybody unable to admit honestly that what we are experiencing is *una sequía* is absolutely deluding herself," she said as she shuttered. "My Tomás, Jr. warned us that we all would pay dearly for our idiotic mistakes." She didn't have to force herself to be reminded that… *'Qui séme le vent récolte la tempête'* [He who sows the whirlwind reaps the storm].

OCHO

'Se lé koulév mouri, ou konn longé lá.' [Only after the serpent is dead are you able to measure it]. This is what *don* Anselmo reminded himself of as he stood alone on the small veranda at the front of his house, hardly able to avoid being reminded of his young warrior-friend Silvio Roumain used to say about the sanctity of life. Anselmo's elegiac remembrance of selective past events was deliberately intended to reexamine certain perceptions about the process of trying to reconstruct community... his former *batey* community, of course. Memory had forever been pivotal to his entire experience, as well as to the collective experience of his former comrades and confidants during their days together at *Esperanza Dulce*. For this holy trinity, remembrance was a solemn step in crossing difficult boundaries of space, time, history, and consciousness in order to reconnect with that sacred world... *'an ba dlo.'*

From his veranda, *don* Anselmo saw a pathetically withered landscape that, according to Silvio, would certainly be in defiance of his *'sanctity of life'* ideal... but now on a grander scale. From his modest veranda, the old man could see on all sides of the house a sight so horrific and so unacceptable that he would not have wished it upon his most treacherous enemy. Where before there always had been his dependable and routinely cared for little *'conuco'* [traditional, small vegetable garden for household consumption]... sprouting the familiar *yucca, jautía* ...both yellow and white varieties-- *berengena, pepinos, ñame, tomates, calabasa*-- that was now a nondescript brown patch of useless, dried weeds without the possibility of being fit for a decent meal. Even the unusually scrawny, resident guinea fowl that could regularly depend on freely helping themselves to a daily meal, seemed startled to find absolutely nothing growing alongside the old man's house. Where there always had been the thick-leaf banana and macaw trees equally swaying scandalously beneath the silky caress of either the early morning or evening breezes were now irregular, motionless stumps. It was as if an angry axman had deliberately engaged in an act of planned vengeance against the old Anselmo by cutting down these glorious trees, thus depriving the old bachelor of ample fruit. Where there always had been a hefty blanket of thorn acacias unfolding their golden blooms along either side of the meandering path leading up toward the picturesque stucco house was now completely barren. How cruel indeed was the sight.

No longer could *don* Anselmo enjoyment of the elongated, elegant stems of the pastel-colored amaryllis with their delicately draped necklaces of bright yellow blossoms; nor could he delight in the sight of playful spider ferns overrunning the banks of the shallow spring bordering his property. Gone altogether was the near magical and cherished anesthesia for him.

"*Carajo*! Damn this barrenness," he was provoked to blurt out. The hidden flock of tiny birds, in a sudden flurry of commotion, were awakened from their daytime slumber as they rushed dizzily from the leafy protection of the flowerless *flamboyán* trees. The frightened creatures scattered in different directions as they were forced to abandon their otherwise comfortable habitat.

"*La maldita sequía* is the true enemy here," he confirmed his angry rebuke to the sky. For him, the present drought crisis was much like one particularly heinous event in the *Isla's* tortured past. Anselmo recalled with clarity and with much agony -- as was his uncanny way of suddenly reaching far back into his neatly archived memory-- the incident itself as if it had occurred only the previous weekend. At that time so long ago, an innocent eight-year-old Anselmo became an orphan immediately when his parents-- a noble, hard-working mother and a respected *'prèt savann'* [country priest]-- in the company of two of little Anselmo's older brothers and two of his uncles on his father's side, were ruthlessly murdered by *El Jefe* [The Chief].

Rafael Leonidas Trujillo, the diabolical, merciless dictator who ruled the eastern side of the *Isla* with iron-clad brutality from 1930 until 1961, when he himself was finally assassinated in a well-planned and executed ambush attack one night. *Don* Anselmo still remembered the much earlier, indiscriminate slaughter of 1937 with torment even after so many years. He continued standing on his veranda, gazing out upon the stark consequences of this on-going *sequía*. His thoughts raced back to that horror as he easily made the emotional connection between those hideous crimes committed then and this present instance of unimaginable dread in the form of the widening drought. The old man's eyes watered.

"So many poor folk were massacred on sight by Trujillo's squads during *"El Corte"*[The Cutting], as we called it, that you couldn't keep count. Many folks weren't even Haitian... they were just Black! That was enough for the marauders who were roaming throughout the border zone day and night. Many folks also stopped believing in the powers of the *Isla's* sacred spirits after what happened"

He closed his old eyes tightly as his crisp memory recalled the horrendous nightmare. The 'Supreme Dictator'– as Trujillo was openly referred to in every corner of the Caribbean and Latin America-- had mounted a superbly orchestrated, evil scheme of ethnic cleansing, a campaign of genocide against the perceived cultural, economic and political threat of the growing presence of Haitians and Dominico-Haitians throughout the bustling border zone. The government itself referred blatantly to the process as *'blanqueamiento'* ['a whitening' or 'bleaching'], ultimately intended for the entire country... or so it was widely thought.

As nearly everybody soon realized, Trujillo's plan initially targeted the black Haitians and Dominicans of Haitian descent living throughout the *'zona fronteriza' [border zone]*, but subsequently caught in the terror trap were hundreds, if not thousands of unsuspecting *bona fide* Dominican citizens whose single 'crime' was their skin color. According to now-acknowledged, verifiable historical records and many scholarly investigations, between 30,000 and 40,000 individuals-- including women, children, and old people-- were massacred in the raids conducted by *El Chivo's* ['the goat', another name for Trujillo] soldiers, para-military squadrons, and eager blood-thirsty thugs drafted into service from local communities in the border zone. In the towns and villages of the countryside, as the old man recalled painfully, victims were usually rounded up and led away before being slaughtered. In many isolated areas, helpless souls were killed in plain sight. Few were shot; instead, machetes, bayonets and thick, wooden clubs were used. This tactic, it was said, reduced the noise that would have alerted more innocent people. According to witnesses of the massacre, many young men and boys, like little Anselmo, were generally separated from their families and then forced to dig mass graves.

These same grave diggers, upon completing their task, were beaten with clubs and then decapitated. Fetuses were ripped savagely from women's bellies; small children were seized by the ankles and had their heads smashed against the nearest rock or tree. Infants were literally tossed into the air only to descend upon waiting bayonets.

Even today, the question is often asked, "How were Haitians and Dominicans identified on sight... especially the children of these two groups?" There was the infamous *'Parsely Test.'* The militia used Spanish pronunciation as a kind of litmus test for deciding 'exactly who was Haitian.' Many soldiers demanded that those captured utter the word *'perejil'* [parsley]... sometimes the word *'tijeras'* [scissors], or other words with the letter *"r"*. The supposed inability to pronounce the Dominican "*r*" was then presented as irrefutable evidence of Haitian identity. As a small boy who managed miraculously to escape '*El Corte*', or as Haitians called the massacre...'*Lé Kout Kouto*'. At the time, little Anselmo could not digest fully the depth of Trujillo's evil. All those gruesome images, though, never left him. Within time, Anselmo would see for himself the correlation between those horrific past deeds; and the present, vengeful *sequí* silently devastating all forms of vegetation everywhere. The violent and deliberate destruction of a community of people, leaving barren the soil as well as the soul of thousands of targeted victims who had committed no offense or transgression against the sacred spirits. The old man now made the emotional connection between those hideous crimes committed then and this present dread; his old eyes watered.

To Anselmo, the thought was without reason. A maniacal dictator whose own maternal grandmother was of Haitian descent-- clearly not European, made the monstrous decision to try to rid the country of all traces of visible blackness... of Africanness. According to Trujillo's perverted thinking... '*all civilized elements and notions of Hispanic and Spanish Christian purity would be allowed to reign supreme and unchallenged, unimpaired against those of non-Christian and African-descended 'savage', uncivilized cultural traditions and values throughout the land, beginning in the 'zona fronteriza.'*

When the old man opened his still moist eyes slowly after reflecting painfully upon that almost surreal past history, he realized that the horror was again visiting his community in the form of '*la maldita sequía.*' He clearly saw the cruel decay of life around him. Alegra had pointed out an undisputed fact.

"Over the last 50 years, developments in agriculture, such as fertilizers and irrigation, have increased yields of the world's staple foods, but we're now beginning to see a slowdown in yield increases. The increasing frequency of excessively hot days across the world could explain some of this slowdown. And feeding a growing population as climate change presents a real challenge, especially since available land for agricultural expansion is limited. Supplies of major food crops could be at serious risk as we plan for future climates."

Her impressive observations were also dramatic and disturbing images that stayed with the old man. His anger was a natural consequence of his many difficult years toiling in the sugarcane fields since the age of seven or eight. His early indomitable warrior spirit, said to be inherited from the god Changó, had been passed down to him from the ancestors. He learned at an early age to disregard quickly the trivia, as his own elders described it, in life's challenging circumstances.

He had said to everyone at the time, "I see the end of sugar announcing something newer for those greedy bosses, but not necessarily sweeter for these piss-poor, already miserable and exploited souls who remain enslaved here in this cesspool of raw, stinking greed."

With each successive year, the old man witnessed sugarcane's unparalleled dominance fade as the rapid development of tourism quickly took its place. He saw the influx of wave after wave of staggering numbers of recruited cheap labor, stream after stream of truck caravans arriving with dangerously overloaded human cargo. This new cargo formed the much needed brigades of construction workers for the new industry.

"*Malé pa gin klaksonn.* Disasters always arrive unannounced," the wise *batey* elder recalled saying as he watched each ominous arrival then. With a feeling of nausea, he muttered another of his calamitous predictions, most always used on occasions that provoked naked rage and disgust.

"*Peyi-ap fini nan lanmè*" [The country is going to end up in the sea]. He was reacting, of course, to what he was learning about the increased havoc from the effects of the *sequía* in different regions of *la Isla*. For instance, amid the searing heat that was scorching the northern provinces in recent weeks, more and more frustrated community groups began to stage protests. Among other things, these outraged and desperate citizens were demanding that the nearby aqueduct and sewage facilities supply more water to their suffering communities. Violent clashes between demonstrators and the *Policía Nacional* were occurring without warning and with greater frequency. The same situation was being repeated in neighboring northwestern provinces. Here, the enraged citizens warned that until the government resolves the water crisis, protests would continue. Chaos and mayhem grew more constant and perilous, seemingly with each passing day without urgently needed water. In local towns, the demonstrators blocked roads, bridges, and crossways with torched vehicle tires, tree trunks, broken bottles and other debris. Before long, the national media began focusing on the wide-spread effects of the drought. The impact was dramatic according to all accounts.

"Raging wildfires are gradually spreading across large sections of the Island's densely forested northern zones. Hundreds of families living in the communities that straddle the path of these suddenly erupting fires are being evacuated with immediate speed for their own safety."

Another report indicated that... *"The National Oceanic and Meteorological Association has observed the highest temperatures on record for the last 50 years across the entire Island. Moreover, the agency is seeking the higher than usual winds and observably rougher ocean waves off our coasts."*

But although the worsening drought crisis was finally attracting nationwide attention, as an infuriated Chelaine earlier had remarked, *"The news editors consistently are refusing to employ the word 'drought' in portraying such graphic events being witnessed throughout the Island."* Truly frightened were the many defenseless families trapped in the paths of Nature's unrelenting onslaught of devastation, along with the accompanying broiling temperatures, were parching the soil and withering crops in all directions. It did not escape the old man's still alert recollection that not so many years ago a landmark heat wave had taken place in Europe; the huge regions of the European continent had suffered the hottest summer in memory. By late summer of that particular year-- *don* Anselmo thought that it may have been in 2003-- news reports indicated that corpses were piling up outside morgues across Paris.

Chelaine had confirmed that such accounts were true. According to her, official estimates of the total death toll reached nearly 72,000 in Europe that year. By the end of the year, *don* Anselmo had learned a new word -- *global warming.'* The term had become a common phrase in news bureaus, government ministries and in ordinary homes around the world. The excessive heat and resulting drought at that time effectively changed the conversation about climate change throughout Europe.

The science adviser to the British government, for example, referred to climate change as... *"the most severe problem we now face during these critical times, for more serious even than the real threat of terrorism."* Elsewhere, it was reported that ... *"By the 2020's, hot days are expected to occur over large areas of France where previously extremely hot days were uncommon, and unless farmers find ways to combat the heat stress that damages seed formation, yields of French maize could fall by 12% compared to today; there will be some differences with other crops in different locations, but extreme heat is not good for crops. One important study showed that global productivity of spring wheat could easily drop by 20% by the 2050s, but such a drop in yields is delayed until perhaps 2100 if concrete measures are taken to cut greenhouse gas emissions."*

In another study, it was found that ... *"River flooding was the impact which was most reduced if climate action is taken. Without action, even optimistic forecasts suggest that the world will warm by 4C, which would expose about 330 million people around the globe to greater flooding. But that number could be cut in half if carbon emissions start to fall in the next few years. Flooding is the biggest climate threat to the US, with over 8,000 homes submerged in 2012."*

From the comfort of his veranda, *don* Anselmo reached his own conclusions. *"Coño!* Right here we're living through our own special Hell because of this *'maldito calentamiento global'* [damned global warming]. This *sequía* is too much to bear and it's bringing misery and worse to millions of our folks. No doubt about it; this is the worst damn heat wave in years-- worse than I can remember. Right now, we're looking at natural disaster zones, and I foresee real violence coming. Damn food prices gonna rise for sure. Who can forget the situation back in 2001, or maybe it was in 2002; food riots broke out across the whole Island."

There were further reports that farmers in one town in the southwestern region of the *Isla* could have revealed, unwittingly, the main reason behind the as yet unexplained growth of *Lago* Enriquillo, the Caribbean's biggest lake, which local residents are describing as *'algo raro'* ...'a strange phenomenon.' The farmers all said they are worried after the appearance of a stream of subsurface water which is flooding their farmland full of crops, and has driven them to the brink of despair. Since the early 1980s the forests in the region have been leveled to make way for crops and needed pasturelands; the soil is subsequently inability to retain the rainwater.

"Este maldito agua está matando el cultivo [This damned water is killing the crops]," all the area farmers echoed in angered puzzlement as the lake steadily got bigger.

The last time *don* Anselmo predicted that the country *"was going to end up in the sea"* was many years ago when the government tried to prepare itself for the massive, bold general strike-- the first of its kind in the Island's history. The decided action had been carefully planned and executed by a determined group of labor activists who were no longer willing to accept the deplorable working conditions and humiliating abuses and exploitation at the height of the

Island's tourism boom. The president himself had fed the population hopes of..."*fantastic levels of materials gains with ambitious proposals for economic growth and promises of untold profits and an overwhelmingly large number of jobs.*"

Such claims, however, proved to be unrealistic for the vast majority of the people, but nevertheless true for a very small cadre of elite investors and policy makers. Tourism, as everybody quickly learned, affected everybody across the Island's social spectrum: from the eager investors in hotel and resort development, whether local or international-- to the urban migrants working in the restaurant and hotel kitchens, dishwashers, cooks, table servers, domestic workers, and even the beach hawkers peddling colorful, but gaudy and useless trinkets, outlandish hats and sunglasses to the tourists on the beaches. To the various categories of employers, then, the planned general strike would adversely impact their vital source of revenue. Moreover, the strike produced an inevitably severe negative effects on foreign investments; also on requirements for loan guarantees from the notorious International Monetary Fund... requirements, of course, which are normally very stringent and regarded as unreasonable. Activists knew that a country's often delicate socio-political climate was crucial for IMF considerations. Azúcar's husband Lucien had made a piercing observation that went almost unnoticed at the time.

"Azúcar, *ma cherie*, do you realize that this strike is set to take place during the very week that the government is scheduled to begin negotiations with the IMF inspectors? And we're talking about that $800 million, two-year standby loan. '*Les saluds!*' [The mindless sons-of-bitches]. Those behind this fuckin' strike should all be castrated."

"*General Strike Paralyzes Island,*" read the headlines at daybreak the morning of the strike. The unavoidable event happened as folks everywhere knew it would. As *don* Anselmo remembered, the call for the crippling work stoppage swept throughout the land much like a terrifying blaze that traditionally would sometimes engulf entire sugarcane fields long ago; sometimes these fires were carefully planned acts of sabotage. He recalled vividly several such conflagrations.

"*Carajo!* If you closed your eyes, you could almost hear the old slave plantation echoing with the angry ghosts of marauding slaves of that period; giant flames leaping from stalk to stalk as frightened field rats darted out between the thick rows of rapidly charring cane." rapidly charring cane."

The strike had been enormously victorious, as everyone saw; more than a few members of the president's cabinet whispered in acknowledgement; many folks in the business sector felt the punitive rage of the workers. Newspaper presses across the *Isla* were shut down, making it impossible to release press updates of the day's swiftly moving events. Without surprise to anyone, the president's response had been equally swift and brutally repressive. There were indiscriminate arrests of hundreds of specifically targeted individuals in strategic areas across the country. Police even arrested some labor activists and supporters merely for distributing fliers promoting the strike. Detainees were never given justifiable reasons for their arrest and detention.

Countless neighborhood and precinct organizers were accused— without the slightest of concrete evidence-- of providing illegal fire arms and ammunition to young delinquents. These young people were also rounded up and arrested. Nearly one hundred civilians were killed by the police and the National Army, with scores more injured during this unprecedented strike that lasted five consecutive days. Led by a fearless and solid coalition of workers from the construction trades, municipal and transport workers, the protestors clashed with greatly outnumbered and heavily armed police and soldiers. The strike, which organizers declared a major success, took a violent turn amid the intimidating military presence. Menacing armored vehicles rumbled out in full strength onto the principal thoroughfares and auxiliary streets of the capital city and other populous cities.

Unidentified demonstrators torched offices of the ruling political party and the State Water and Sewers Ministry, the State Revenue Ministry, as well as a prominent branch office of the Central Commercial Bank. However, most remarkably there were no reported incidents involving foreign visitors or tourists during the disturbances; on the previous evening of the announced strike, the president had very thoughtfully dispatched special army tactical units to guard the major tourism compounds throughout the Island's tourist zones. Totally blinded by reality, the head of the armed forces had insisted from the start that "the situation was under control." There was no doubt that naked fear gripped the entire population. For the duration of this violent and dangerous episode, to old *don* Anselmo's mind was that same recurring premonition that...

"Peyi-ap fini nan lanmè" [The country is going to end up in the sea].

NUEVE

Don Anselmo's ominous prediction notwithstanding, the thought of the clearly spiteful wrath of the sacred spirits being unleashed upon so many thousands of innocent souls was much more than a mere idle curiosity for the scientifically-minded Alegra. She felt quite differently because the scope of the crisis was so massive. She was thoroughly convinced that the *sequía* now plaguing various global landscapes, in addition of course to those in the *Isla* of her birth, was in its early stages. For her, the later and far more severe levels in the destructive process were yet to come. But the alert young climatologist knew all too well that the total force of the devastation would definitely catch everyone unprepared. It was exactly as old *don* Anselmo had relentlessly warned folks over so many years earlier that it would happen ...Perhaps he was not at all surprised.

At the same time, though, Alegra Saint Jacques was almost equally consumed by a dramatically different kind of alarm. "The alarm" in this instance, however, arrived in the form not of any physical manifestation, but rather one that was more subtle, more excitingly new and strange for her. It was quite an emotional alarm pulsating noticeably deep inside her. And it had absolutely nothing to do with 'ancient ancestral spirits', as she convinced herself. There was no mistake about it; Alegra had lived a life that, until most recently, had been sheltered and jealously protected. Since her early adolescence, that life had followed a very narrow, restricting course that could only be described as cloistered... and by deliberate intension. Her parents, almost from the moment of the child's birth, wanted to impose certain carefully designed safeguards around their daughter's daily life. For the most part, Azúcar and Lucien, as any other loving and well-meaning parents, were convinced that all sorts of dangers, whether imagined or real, were forever present and lurking along their daughter's path. Also, the couple's distinctive socio-political and economic circumstance, in their mind, fully justified the extraordinary precautions taken to shield their little *princesa* against any possible harm. She was, for example, the only pupil attending the *'liceo'* [elite private academy] who arrived and departed daily in a chauffeured, bullet-proof limousine.

Moreover, she was regularly accompanied by an adult chaperone... usually one of the trusted household employees instructed to wait for the little girl directly outside the entrance of every classroom that the child attended throughout the day. At first, her classmates-- all of whom were of equal status in every sense of privilege, ridiculed this rather unusual sight, but which very soon became oblivious to the practice. Not a single other parent of the attending pupils at the academy engaged in this excessive display of protectiveness. At precisely two o'clock each afternoon the same limousine would be waiting to escort the *princesa* and her chaperon back into the welcoming shelter of *La Morenita*.

"Por mi madre, what could I have possibly done to deserve this punishment?" Alegra was puzzled when she once asked herself this question, not fully understanding why her parents-- as sweet and loving as they were--- nevertheless were always so insistent upon having her watched every moment of the day.

"Why do they treat me like this, especially since they must know that I'd never do anything to disgrace them in any way? I'm no longer a baby; don't they realize how terribly embarrassing this makes me feel?"

Such questions used to gnaw at her quite often during her adolescent years. Now as a young woman, however, she began to understand the genuine concern and protectiveness of her parents. But these were not the questions that stirred the young woman's deeper personal emotions, prompting her to venture into the alter room one day... and unaccompanied.

Just as her mother had done as a young girl, so did Alegra also begin her private visits to this special ceremonial room; everybody referred affectionately to this sacred space as 'Mamá Lola's altar room.' At first, Alegra had always been in the company of someone older... whether her mother, her great-grandmother Mamá Lola herself, or one of the household staff. Quite strangely, she used to wonder, but never dared to ask, why her father never went into the room with her. This ornately decorated alter room, upon unchallenged urgency of Mamá Lola, had been incorporated into Lucien's original design and ultimate construction of *La Morenita*; it was discreetly tucked alongside the spacious linen closet located immediately adjacent to the old woman's bedroom. She had wanted that an altar room be placed in this spot along the long central corridor conveniently connecting the main living area of the house with her private suite so that there would be easy access into the sanctuary by the entire *La Morenita* household for undisturbed prayer and solemn meditation. But unlike many other deeply religious persons who simply reserved a special prayer corner in their home, the old woman would never have dreamt of keeping the door to this room locked. Anyone at any time, during the course of the day or evening, was always free to enter.

What provoked Alegra's entry into Mamá Lola's altar room was the now clear feeling that this young scientist harbored for a particular young man... also a scholar and colleague at the university. She had used the single adjective '*captivating*' to describe him. Alegra was prepared to admit to herself while alone in the privacy of the altar room that she was in love. Being there, in all honesty, had nothing whatsoever to do with any suspected or conflicted feelings about her religiosity. The only thing that the young first-year co-ed thought about was that "*Nelson Campos de la Rosa was stunningly exotic.*"

Moreover, it wasn't so much that he was *latino* and came from the sun-drenched shores of the Caribbean... as she would later learn. The university was remarkably diverse in terms of ethnicity, religion, nationality and gender identity. In fact, the admissions office prided itself in having an impressive number of Latinos among its student and faculty populations. Regarding Campos de la Rosa's physical appearance, it was his immediate 'eye-candy attractiveness' that garnered him the description of being 'stunningly exotic.'

The first time that Alegra saw him among the varsity squad of the university's soccer team ...which was a rather unusual accomplishment for a first-year athlete on scholarship, the young co-ed was 'captivated' by Nelson's exceptional handsomeness. He had amazingly deep-set, large black eyes that were shaded by long, thick black lashes --unusually lengthy for a guy, she thought. His large, alert eyes were of the kind that actually seemed to dart constantly and quickly from one focal point to the next within his surroundings. The quick movement of his eyes reminded Alegra of those same alert eyes of the many tropical birds she remembered from her early years at *La Morenita*. Her mysterious soccer player had a heavy stock of jet black, curly hair that hung low and seductively into his lively black eyes.

Alegra couldn't be certain at first if Nelson's eyes eyes were capricious or flirtatious or simply 'active', she admitted with curiosity. His smooth complexion was a rich tropical *'trigueño'*, which would best be described as a kind of perpetually dark-colored wheat. His teeth were large and even, with a brilliant whiteness that sparkled dramatically under his razor-thin black mustache. Mostly, his features were broad and rough, not at all chiseled; the nose, cheeks, and chin were manly like those of a well- toned college athlete; he was effortlessly captivating in every conceivable regard. In total honesty, Alegra had never been one of those traditionally frivolous --in her words-- adolescent girls who routinely chatter among themselves about having a *'novio'*[boyfriend] one week, before dismissing him by the weekend, before deciding upon another one by Monday. To the contrary, *'pura inocencia'* [pure innocence] would most accurately describe Alegra even at this stage in her development as a young woman attending university so far from home.

Therefore, to her inexperienced and purely innocent mind, the notion of 'spectacular' suggested exactly that. 'Spectacular', she decided, described Nelson's lips. The feature about Nelson, more so than anything else, that overwhelmed her untested and purely erotic sensibilities was this young man's full, fleshy, and sensuous lips, encasing a wide mouth. Such lips on a man she had seen before, but only on celebrities from '*telenovelas*' [TV soap operas] or the movies or in magazines...'*Labios dulces*' [sweet lips] was the commonly-heard term all the Spanish-speaking co-eds used in referring to Nelson's lips, certainly not the disparaging term '*bembón*' that some consciously racist *latinos* use to ridicule the over-hanging, lower lip of some of the *Isla*'s fellow citizens of African descent. There are even popular songs that intentionally ridicule '*el bembón*'.

Alegra thought secretly, "Nelson's delicious lips are those that I would definitely not hesitate in inviting to plant wet kisses on my welcoming mouth."

"Miss Ferrand Saint Jacques, if you have a few minutes, I'd like to introduce you to a fellow student who I think is from the same Caribbean island as you," said Alegra's geology professor --one of her favorites-- after class one afternoon. "He should be waiting in my office as we speak. Come along and you two hopefully can become acquainted."

"Awesome," Alegra replied with a hint of excitement. Of course, she hadn't the slightest idea who this 'fellow Caribbean' could be. "I'm always very happy to meet a fellow '*caribeño*' [person who is native to the Caribbean region]. Our Island is so small that I wouldn't be surprised if our families actually know one another."

Much to Alegra's delight, there was a better than average representation of students from various islands of the Caribbean. Many of these diligent and deserving young folks were attending the university under the auspices of various kinds of scholarships or sponsorships, whether academic or athletic. Still others had come through the efforts of their parents' very comfortable financial circumstance. Upon arriving at the professor's office, Alegra's professor led her into the spacious room where wide skylights permitted the radiant afternoon mountain sun to drench the entire room. Polished wood-grain walls were lined with imposing floor-to-ceiling bookshelves. There were countless photos of geological expedition teams smiling triumphantly, an array of framed certificates in three or four different languages and impressive awards and plaques adorned one complete wall. There were also mounted snapshots of recognizable and some not so familiar world sites; there were rock samples and climate maps of different sizes and several globes on display. Very simply, it was immediately evident to Alegra that she had entered the sanctuary of a seasoned world explorer and renowned international scholar. Piles of papers, documents, and opened reference books were scattered randomly on the professor's massive oak desk.

Seated with quiet reserve on the visitor's bench located in front of an expansive picture window was the young student who was scheduled to meet with the professor. The young man stood up instantly as if on cue-- but more correctly, of course, as a matter of learned etiquette and decorum. Alegra didn't have to guess if this young man was from the Caribbean; his demeanor said it all rather clearly.

The professor spoke first and directly to the point. "Very good, young man. I see you've come early. Nelson Campos de la Rosa, I'd like to introduce you to another very diligent student of mine, and also like yourself, majoring in world geography and climatology. And by the way, she's originally from the Caribbean ... I believe from the same island."

In that very instant, Alegra felt that her otherwise constantly observant eyes were betraying her... playing a kind of punitive hoax on her exposed sensibilities. She wondered aloud... perhaps even fearing that the other two individuals in the room would hear her. She also wondered if they could hear her heart pulsating. The handsome young man was indeed the very same 'captivating' Adonis to whom she had fallen victim upon first seeing him on that particular afternoon when her friends persuaded her to go with them to the soccer field... where all the hottest jocks could be seen dripping seductively in sweat. Even for the scientifically-minded Alegra, the scene was truly erotic.

Now in the professor's office, she waited for the reserve young man to announce himself with 'traditional, rather staid, Caribbean politeness.'

"Nelson Campos de la Rosa *a su orden, señorita.* [Nelson Campos de la Rosa, at your service, Miss]; it's my sincere pleasure to meet you."

"Al contrario, Nelson Campos de la Rosa" [On the contrary], as she quickly decided to respond in Spanish, *"El placer es mío"* [The pleasure is mine].

If this classic scene had unfolded on the *Isla* during an earlier, long-faded era, Alegra Instinctively have lowered her head slightly forward, smiled demurely before curtseying. But she didn't, of course. She didn't exactly know why she chose to answer in Spanish; perhaps it was merely a reciprocated, impulsive reaction to Nelson's stately civility.

"My name is Alegra Ferrand Saint Jacques. Maybe you might know my family, Azúcar Ferrand, my mother? My father was Lucien Saint Jacques... he's now deceased. I'm absolutely thrilled to meet someone from the same *Isla*."

She didn't exactly know why she chose to answer in Spanish; it could merely have been a reciprocated, impulsive reaction to Nelson's impressive civility. It would have been disingenuous of Nelson not to have recognized the illustrious Ferrand Saint Jacques name. Indeed, anyone living on the Island today-- especially anyone with even a casual awareness of the socio-economic and political issues affecting the daily lives of everybody there-- would be very familiar with everything that the name symbolized. The total economic development of the *Isla* over recent decades has been intricately linked with the name Ferrand Saint Jacques.

"Of course, I know the name," Nelson admitted without displaying an iota of personal sentiment. "However, I don't think our families have actually met, as far as I'm aware. My parents certainly would have mentioned such an occasion and also that we were both studying here at the same university."

Nelson deliberately did not bother to mention that one of his older brothers, along with an uncle, had actually met Alegra's mother. The occasion had been some years ago while Nelson was still in primary school. At the time, the entire *Isla* was experiencing the agony of a crippling workers' strike that quickly turned into a *'paro general'* [general strike]. The country paralyzed every facet of the daily labor activity. Nelson's brother had been an ardent participant in that event; his uncle was savagely beaten by members of the special Anti-Riot Unit of *'La Policía Nacional'* [National Police]. It had been Alegra's mother who had intervened forcefully to prevent further atrocities against the strikers. Nelson made a judicious decision not to reveal to Alegra nor to the professor the exact personal connection that the young man held with his compatriot's family. He sensed that this was not the moment to do so. But before long, Alegra would learn much more about the captivating scholar-athlete.

Acting aggressively, Alegra's new *'amigo'* from the Caribbean made the next calculated move by seizing the opportunity of this propitious meeting to invite her to join him for coffee after class the very next day. Alegra suspected that she would forever be grateful to their mutually shared geology professor for insisting that his prize student accompany him back to his office that particular afternoon. Of course, however, *don* Anselmo, Mamá Lola, and most especially *doña* Fela would have had a great deal to say about this encounter. It was truly far from being coincidental.

DIEZ

It wasn't very long afterwards that the young couple began seeing more and more of each other, naturally becoming better acquainted in matters of character, thoughts, feelings, likes and dislikes of the other. Whether enjoying regular, afternoon coffee dates together in the student center canteen, or spending more serious, concentrated study sessions lasting sometimes more than a few hours, Alegra and Nelson found themselves sharing more and more of the same space. As a result, they ultimately learned important aspects of the other's personality that otherwise would not have been disclosed. Their fortuitous meeting that particular afternoon in the geology professor's office would prove to be driven entirely by predestination— or at least as the *'sabio viejo' don* Anselmo, and also Alegra's venerate great-grandmother *doña* Fela would have explained that fateful encounter in their distinctive traditional fashion, *"Lwa mwen, aprè Papa Ogou, m' se sou kont ou"* [My spirits, after Papa Ogou, I am in your hands] It could not have been more plain than that, according to the two wise elders.

Much to Nelson's delight, his new companion also had now become a loyal and regular fan seated in the bleachers at his soccer practices. Moreover, she never missed any scheduled matches with opposing teams playing on the home field. In the classes they shared, the two had begun to sit next to each other. If for whatever reason one or the other arrived late to class, all their classmates present quickly learned that the empty seat was automatically reserved for the late arriving partner. Routinely, the couple was seen strolling together, hand-in-hand, across campus toward whatever destination. After sharing so much time together on campus, they soon altered the venue by deciding to have dinner one evening during the weekend when there were no scheduled soccer match.

To Alegra's surprise, Nelson chose a trendy Ethiopian restaurant located downtown. The restaurant was popular with the university's vibrant international community. Alegra could not hide her excitement of her companion's sophisticated choice.

"*Ay, por mi madre,*" she exclaimed, "I've wanted to eat here for the longest time, but could never convince my roommates or any of the other girls to come here with me; I didn't want to come alone to a place so elegant."

"*A tu órden.* [At your service], "Nelson answered with unrehearsed charm. The meal itself was truly Ethiopian in every regard, with an ambiance that was far from being bogus. The low, knee-high, round-shaped traditional table with cushioned floor- seating mats would easily have diners imagine they were in the high plateau of Addis Ababa, Ethiopia's ancient capital city. Much to Alegra's gastronomic excitement, the meal began with a typical appetizer-- '*sambus*', which is a fried minced beef patty, with a tantalizing mixture of ginger, cinnamon and onions, folded into a thin crust and fired a golden brown. There was the familiar tomato '*fitfit*'-- diced tomatoes, onions and *jalapeño* pepper mixed with pieces of '*injera*' [flat bread]; Ethiopian-style lentils with baked yam. The entrée was succulent lamb sautéed in a traditional garlic and sweet onion sauce. Most unusual was the drink that Nelson ordered...the honey wine called '*tej*', made from fermented honey and a special kind of hops called '*gesho.*'

"A totally incomparable experience," Alegra said later to her captivating host. By the time they finished their exquisite meal, followed by a cup of thick, aromatic Ethiopian coffee, the gently falling rain outside had now become a menacing downpour. From the window of the restaurant, the diners could see people hurrying in all directions for the nearest offering of possible shelter.

"I hope you enjoyed the meal as much as I did," Nelson said with delight as he sat back on his oversized cushion... secretly gratified with his triumph.

"Not a single complaint," Alegra replied in honesty. "I found myself smiling as I was eating those delicious *'sambusas'* appetizers. They immediately made me think about our tasty *'pastelillos'* back home. Our cook used to have a few waiting for me almost every afternoon when I came home from school. *Mami* was always afraid that those snacks would spoil my dinner later." She laughed aloud.

"Tell me, Alegra, do you miss being home?" Nelson was curious to know.

"To admit the truth, yes, at times. As you know, we are so very far from home. "She remembered how her mother often told stories about her own experiences being in Canada. Some of these stories were terrifying for a young girl like born in the *batey* and never before having traveled even to the *Isla's* capital city. Other accounts, as Alegra recalled about her mother's initial experiences in Canada were quite funny. She again burst into laughter as she and Nelson shared her mother's introduction to the distant city with a name that sounded like *'toronja'* [grapefruit]. Of course, this strange-sounding city was Toronto. They both roared zestfully and ordered more coffee.

As the long and undeniably lovely evening grew longer, so too did the rain grow more prolonged and considerably more intense. It was Nelson's idea, therefore, not to attempt returning to campus during such menacing weather. Visibility was reduced to near zero. It was without exaggeration that the mountain roads leading to the university would be treacherous, especially in the blackness of night with only the car headlights to serve as guide. Was this circumstance another willful act of the forever watchful and protective spirits? Would these two young protagonists become willing players in the rapidly unfolding saga?

"Quite ironic this is," observed Alegra, without being prompted. "Here we are stopped in our tracks by this awful downpour... a thunderstorm and in the very instant our own little *Isla* is experiencing the worst recorded drought that anybody can remember." Her astute and rather provocative comment moved Nelson to reflect upon his companion's observation.

"How right you are, Alegra. *Coño,* only last week I had an email from my brother, and besides chatting about mundane family matters, practically everything else he talked about had to do with the *sequía.* He told me that most people are seriously preoccupied with the terribly damaging effects of the drought. My brother, by the way, lectures at the *Universidad Nacional* in the capital and said that the entire Science and Technology Department there is worried about the higher than normal temperatures throughout the *Isla.* The scientists are also monitoring very closely the rougher ocean waves. The dryness everywhere is reaching critical proportions." Alegra offered additional reporting that she had received from home.

"*Mami* told me not too long ago that there is increasing alarm by almost everyone about what can only be described as 'boiling temperatures'. As a result, the soil is becoming more parched and crops everywhere are withering."

It was well past eleven o'clock and the heavy rain outside had not let up in the least; the couple decided with mutually that it would be more prudent to spend the night in town rather than risk venturing back to campus in the worsening storm. They found a nearby quality motel, one of many conveniently located in the downtown hub, as is common in most college towns. It wasn't even necessary to register falsely as 'Mr. and Mrs.' since the university itself was the focal point of irrefutable liberalism in every respect.

Despite the burdensome rain, the entire evening, Nelson felt, was concluding on a definite note of splendor. Or what is 'achievement' for him? As for Alegra, she was also very much in agreement with her companion's assessment on both accounts. She convinced him without a hint of subtlety that she too was thinking about the evening's brilliance …despite the unforgiving rain outside. Both individuals almost simultaneously conveyed to each through the unmistakable sparkle in their eyes the mutuality of precisely how they desired for this truly enchanted evening not to end. As an adolescent back in the Island attending the lyceum, Alegra wasn't the least bit curious-- as nearly all the other girls most surely were—about matters of sex. Her obsessive curiosity related only to science, especially geography. Moreover, her traditional religious instruction had an almost frightening affect upon her secret notions about sexuality.

To this very day, she could recall having to recite regularly... *"Food for the stomach and the stomach for food; the body is not meant for sexual immorality, but for the Lord, and the not meant for sexual immorality, but for the Lord, and the Lord for the body."* She had been carefully taught to ... *"Flee from sexual immorality"* and that... *"Your body is a temple of the Spirit, who is in you, whom you have received from God."* She, like all the other young pupils, both boys and girls at the *'liceo'* heard constantly from *'las monjas'* [nuns] and *'los padres'* [the priests], as well as from laypersons at the school... "There must not be even a hint of sexual immorality nor of any kind of impurity." In fact, all the pupils had been required to chant as though a mantra and in unison, every afternoon upon finishing their academic lessons... *"It is God's will that I should be sanctified; that I should avoid sexual immorality; that I should learn to control my own body in a way that is hoy and honorable, not in any passionate lust like the heathen."*

For whatever odd reason, Alegra always disliked what she regarded as 'an unnecessary afternoon ritual.' To her, it seemed like having to put on this last piece of protective armor before leaving the sanctity of the *'monjas'* and *'padres'*, and of course, the easily intimidating *'Madre Superiora'*... with all of whom she had spent the excessively long day. Terrifying thoughts indeed! This was rather uncomfortable for an ingenuous, closely guarded Alegra at the time.

The same could rightfully be said for Nelson, although he didn't attend an elite parochial school as Alegra had. To the contrary, his was a public school totally divorced from any degree of religiosity and ritual. In fact, none of his teachers were nuns or priests as in the case with the entire instructional staff at Alegra's lyceum. Nevertheless, both Nelson and Alegra shared immeasurable similarities and patterns of thinking regarding sex. Genuine scientific curiosity and fiercely competitive soccer dominated overwhelmingly young Nelson's coming-of-age experiences. His primary explorations were along the paths of geography-- the same as Alegra-- and of course soccer. Both individuals, therefore, now successfully embarking upon serious university careers, find themselves somewhat conflicted. Alegra seemed more so as she lumbered awkwardly down this unsure road of naked sexual pleasure. She, for instance, did not remember ever hearing that... *"Love is kind; it does not envy, it does not boast."*

Nelson, for his part, was altogether oblivious of the universal truism that... *"Love never fails."* It was unfortunate that neither of them had ever experienced the privilege and joy of sitting at the knee of a *batey* elder so that they might learn these or any vital lessons of life.

In the motel room that stormy night, as she would confess much later, Alegra certainly did not feel herself to be a 'heathen' of any kind, despite her passionate lust at this moment for Nelson. In turn, Nelson felt equally impassioned. Their love-making immediately lost any kind of clumsiness or embarrassing discomfort. Not in the least surprising, instead, their intimacy quickly became 'natural' for both; it was delicate and tender; it was sweet, unimaginably pleasurable and mutually welcomed. Alegra did not feel impure, dishonorable, or immoral. What was 'immoral' anyway? She always wanted to ask the *'monjas'*, but of course, never dared. Nelson was like a gallant expert.

"Mi dulce amor [My sweet love], how many more secret treasures of sweetness and love are hidden behind those beautiful brown eyes of yours?" he insisted of his declared lover.

Alegra felt her virgin heart palpitating gingerly; she did not want Nelson to release her nor to extract his deliciousness from inside her. It dizzied her mind to know that she was being held in the amorous grip of a man for the very first time in her life... at the age of nineteen. Back at the *'liceo'*, her female classmates, but also a few boys, would often ridicule her for not having had any experimentation with sex as so many of them indeed had. However, these taunts never seemed to bother the future climate scientist. She could hear the pounding rain outside rapidly becoming harder with each drop. She allowed herself to be pleasantly conquered by the tender force of Nelson's seductive advances. Like cool Caribbean breezes at night, Nelson's sweet words of desire blew into Alegra's receptive ear.

"*Mi dulce Alegrita,* don't be afraid of your heart; please let me be the only one to intensify the natural sweetness of your spirit ... not just tonight, but every single night from now on." His sensuous lips planted honeyed kisses on her firm breasts. He kissed her smooth neck and shoulders; the innocent, vanquished Caribbean climate student was ready, and thus very carefully assisted Nelson's gentle entry into the temple. She reflected to herself, "*I shall now know fully, even as I am fully known. And now there remain faith, hope and love... the greatest of these being love.*"

This preciously intimate act of love happening on this rainiest of nights in a university town so far away from home would be only the beginning of many a delicious night yet to come for the two innocent young scientists from the same little *Isla caribeña*. The rain outside did not seem to want to stop falling.

ONCE

Back on the *Isla*, it still had not rained for three hundred and thirty-one days continuously. The blistering hot temperatures in as many days were far above normal, displaying little or no evidence of pause or cessation. The accompanying *sequía* was merciless. The *Isla*'s long fabled resplendence of consistently lush, green foliage was rapidly vanishing. It was not necessary that *don* Anselmo be convinced by learned climatologists that... *"climate change poses an indisputable threat to civilization itself."* The former *batey* elder could see as well as feel for himself the horrendous effects of the increasing 'atmospheric disturbances.'

"Kalfou danjere! Dangerous crossroads," he mused aloud, easily recalling all that he had been taught so long ago about the nature of things. *"O zanj nan dlo.* Oh Angels in the water." His agonizing plea transported him directly back to a time when he used to have a strangely recurring dream ...a dream with a particularly hypnotic song, that at least to the old man, contained rather mystical lyrics. According to traditional Vodou lore, Gran Oyá is the rapturously beautiful enchantress from the land of the dead, *mpemba*. She regularly stands in the middle of a stream at night, combing her long hair while singing. Her deceptively sweet voice lures the bewitched on-shore listener into the stream at the spot where she waits before seducing him to follow her deep beneath the water, never to be seen again.

In the old man's dream, both he and Grand Oyá sing the song together; he was never able to erase that mesmerizing song from his memory.

... *"M'domi, m'reve sou lan m'te ye, Zetoiles leve grand jou*
... *M' domi, m'reve nam pays-m m'te ye;*
... *Soleil chaire lan nuite, L'heu-a rive."*

… [I slept, I dreamed that I was below the sea;
… Stars rose with the dawning day. I slept, I dreamed that I was in
… My homeland; the sun shone in the darkness of night to say:
… The time has arrived.]

As haunting as it was, that song revealed to him the 'other side' [*an ba dlo*-- that sacred place where the ancient spirits dwell]... that place where human souls go for a period of exactly one year and a day immediately after the soul dies. During those times in the *batey*, everyone always believed this without question; they just did. However, now there was doubt. *Don* Anselmo couldn't be certain given the many modern changes that had taken place all around him since those days. At any rate, his dream had to do with the scared passage between life and death; that was the vital importance of the water in everybody's life. For him, as well as for everybody else, life and death are symbolized by *'agua'*.

Alarmingly, as the *batey* elder was witnessing for the past three hundred and thirty-one days, it had not rained a single drop. Most of the *Isla*'s streams and brooks, even several of the minor rivers had become ugly, cracked beds of hard, dry clay. The distance between life and death was narrowing dangerously ... in some case, this distance had disappeared altogether.

"*Carajo!* Mayanèt in all her infamous and often merciless toughness has dealt us the maximum vengeance. There's also been a heavy dosage of irony accompanying her calculated scheme," Anselmo insisted, with no one else listening as witness to his anger. He suspected that Mayanèt was probably smiling with smug satisfaction at this sudden turn of events regarding the local eco-systems now becoming more and more directly impacted by the unbelievable deterioration all around him

Ever since the mournful departure of several of cherished comrades who formed the hallowed trinity in the intricately interlaced lives of both *Don* Anselmo and Azúcar, the two old friends were now sharing more frequent visits than previously. It must be remembered that the old man had known Azúcar's grandmother since well before Azúcar was born. The two had shared the very painful loss of Azúcar's only true love-- her husband Lucien. Then there was the loss of Lucien's trusted friend and confidant, León Dumas ... best buddies since their university days together in Toronto; other great losses included Madame Yvette Origène-Desgraves, Lucien's long-anonymous benefactress and strident advocate for socio-economic reforms on the *Isla*; gone also was Mamá Lola, Lucien's grandmother; and of course, one of the most mournful losses, the *batey's* most revered living saint at the time, *doña* Fela.

Like everybody else without fail, *don* Anselmo and Azúcar opened their conversation by routinely commenting on what they saw as a steadily encroaching *sequía* all around them. There was a noticeable rise in sea levels with warmer ocean temperatures, increasing thunder storms followed by tidal surges, the unusual flooding produced by heavier torrential rains, the frightful mud-slides in higher elevations of the countryside during periods of fierce rains... the overall vengeful climate. Azúcar even shared with her old friend the official notices of the rapid melting of Arctic ice caps and glaciers ... located so very far away from their little Caribbean *Isla* that those ice caps might as well have been situated on the other side of the moon. With each successive visit, it wasn't difficult for Anselmo and his hostess to find themselves spending the entire day together discussing any number of mutual concerns.

Don Anselmo was anxious, for instance, to hear about Alegra's academic progress ... especially since she had traveled so far from home to study about what the old man described simply as '*weather and climate.*' According to his unique way of looking at this, '*el sabio*' felt that "*all that you possibly needed to learn about the weather and climate you could gather from direct, careful observation of nature itself.*" Studying the movement of the stars at night, he felt, or following the rises and falls of the daily ocean tides, or paying close attention to the drift of the clouds and their distinct shapes, or being mindful of the warmth of the ocean's surface and the moisture in the air currents could tell you everything about *'el tiempo y el clima'* [weather and climate]. After all, he himself had thoroughly learned such necessary things from the trusted *batey* elders when he was still a young boy cutting sugarcane alongside many of those 'old wise ones.'

However, he would certainly not deny the genuine pride he felt in knowing that little Alegrita wanted to learn so much more about nature by attending university classes just as her mother had done, even if it meant going far away from the *Isla* to do so. The young woman's mother explained in easy fashion for her honorable old friend the nature of climate science and her daughter's passion for this challenging and provocative study.

Azúcar was equally excited about sharing with her honorable friend her daughter's recently awakening love concerns. On several occasions following the young couple's memorable dinner date a certain rainy night, mother and daughter had literally spent hours chatting on the phone about the latest episode in what was unmistakably a budding romance between the two university classmates from the same *Isa*. Azúcar was convinced that for her admittedly naive and previously shattered *princesa*, each new episode was more intriguing than the last one reported.

Don Anselmo wanted to know more about Alegra's young suitor. Her mother offered what she thought was sufficient information to satisfy the old man's curiosity.

"*Qué bendición de Dios!* What a blessing from God! The young man is from right here...from our *Isla*. Although I don't know the family at all, I do feel confident that he is a fine young man and comes from a respectable family ... *a family of quality*. According to Alegra, he is also on government sponsorship and a champion soccer player. In fact, he was the outstanding captain of the national team representing our *Isla* at the recent Olympic Games. Of course, though, as I said, I don't know exactly who his parents are."

Azúcar couldn't have been a prouder mother exhibiting unapologetic enthusiasm for a daughter's happiness, but with a hint of noticeable irritability. However, the old man took particular issue with his hostess's edginess regarding the young soccer player's *'abolengo'* [lineage]. Azúcar couldn't have been more transparent... or perhaps 'shallow' on this point.

"*Que todos los santos nos protejan m'hijita* [May all the saints protect us, my dear child]. Is knowing who the boy's family is that important to you, Azúcar?" the old man asked in genuine dismay. He was noticeably perturbed by his dear friend's description of Alegra's young suitor; *don* Anselmo wasn't capable of masking his feelings under any circumstances. He almost didn't recognize this portrait of his long-standing friend from the *batey*.

"*Coño!* What in hell is that all about? A *respectable* family? A family of class?"

This was in no way reflective of his young *'azúcar morenita'* [little lump of brown sugar] whom everybody back in the *batey* always knew as that unpretentious and fearless champion of workers' right during those heady days of labor unrest at the height of tourism expansion on the *Isla* and the aftermath of significant labor reforms. The old man knew that neither his dear friend nor her husband Lucien would ever have chosen to use such disdainful terms in describing other folk.

"*Mi querida hijita, ¿qué te pasa?* My dear child, what's the matter with you?" he wanted to know.

"*Por el amor de todos los santos.* [For the love of all the saints.] How I wish *abuelita* were here now to offer me the guidance I so desperately need regarding my little *princesa*."

Anselmo could hear the agony in this mother's voice. "His name is Nelson Campos de la Rosa and from what I understand, he is the *Isla*'s national *fútbol* [soccer] champion on scholarship in the U.S.A… in Colorado. Surprisingly, one of his older brothers had also been one of our national stars when he signed a lucrative contract to play professionally in Spain. Alegra never talks about the young man's family-- only that they come from one of those newly developed industrial municipalities in the *'zona fronteriza'*.

Don Anselmo was familiar with several of the many towns that constitute the epicenter of the *Isla's* booming duty free, export-processing and assembly plants that had been established in the border zone. These towns now dot the country's rural areas that were once historic settlements for Dominican-Haitians. He had actually visited a few of these towns and knew them well enough. The old man was also knowledgeable about the traditional pattern of family names… especially in the former sugarcane zones. Precisely in Nelson's case, as in so many other cases like his, *don* Anselmo knew that the attached *'de la Rosa'* to a family's surname usually signaled that a deliberate alteration had been made to conceal a prior identity; it wasn't necessarily due to some kind of possible criminality, but nevertheless an undesirable taint whereupon that family's otherwise respectable name had been somehow sullied by scandal or shame. Thus, the name *'Campos de la Rosa'* [Fields of Roses] cleverly suggested the 'sweetness and luster' of a field of roses.

"There had been a cleansing of some kind," the old man thought to himself. Azúcar would not have known of the practice because it fell into disuse before she was born and so the custom had long been buried securely in the *Isla's* traditions by then; most people simply forgot all about the specific origins of the name. Anselmo was curious, perhaps even a bit suspicious about the need or the desire on the part of the young man's family to make that change. When Azúcar described for the old man the physical appearance of her daughter's heart-throb, *don* Anselmo's keenly instinctive inquisitiveness heightened considerably. How had Alegra painted her soccer star?

"*Extraordinarily handsome with deep-set, large dark eyes that were constantly darting all around his surroundings ... eyelashes that were thick and black, really quite lengthy for a man; heavy stock of black, shiny, curly hair that hung seductively low into his eyes; his complexion was a rich, dark-colored wheat [called 'trigueño' in the Caribbean]; beautiful, sparkling-white, large teeth; broad and rough features, with fleshy lips encasing a wide mouth that seemed even wider when he smiles his captivating smile.*"

The constantly alert '*viejo sabio del batey*' [wise old man from the *batey*] nearly chocked on the gulp of coffee he was sipping, his cup poised in mid-air as if suddenly paralyzed by an invisible, but formidable insect sting... or perhaps by a penetrating bolt of electrifying revelation. Such unexpected reaction could hardly have gone unnoticed by his hostess seated directly opposite him. Anselmo honestly thought that he had just listened to the precisely painted portrait of a certain ghost from *Esperanza Dulce's* distant, often ugly past. Without the slightest difficulty, he was able to break through the misty haze of history... the unforgettable face of a man who used to invoke automatic revulsion and loathing in every corner of the *batey*.

"*Pero, por dios, don Anselmo, qué le pasa?*" What's the matter? Are you alright?" Azúcar inquired urgently. Slowly placing the coffee cup on the small table separating the two, the old man looked directly into her widened eyes and uttered the long forbidden two words... '*Mario Montalvo*'. There was an unmistakable tone of dread in Anselmo's old voice.

"*M'hijita*, we must go right this instant into the sacred altar room. '*Se on ki pou mété lod lan sa!*' [We are the ones who will straighten things out]."

Azúcar recalled this all too familiar expression from their shared past; it was always heard in moments of much personal or collective conflict. Anselmo was saying that the two of them, he and she together, would have to sift through everything put before them, subsequently arriving at reasonable explanations and a convincing conclusion. Naturally, of course, the task would be accomplished with the solicited aid of the sacred ancestral spirits. Azúcar, still fully cognizant and without question deeply respectful of the 'ways of the elders', obeyed without question or hesitation…"We must consult the sacred *'lwas'*; let us hurry without delay," he added.

As was part of the long-practiced ritual, the old man first knocked softly, three times on the unlocked door; this was to rouse the spirits inside, announcing his arrival. Once inside the room, Anselmo knew next to light three white candles… a small stack of these was placed on a table alongside the interior wall. Next, he took a bottle of *'kleren'* [raw sugarcane rum] that was also found on the table with the box of candles; he poured exactly three drops of the strong rum onto the floor. This was the traditional libation as an offering to Papa Legba, guardian of the entrance to the realm of the sacred spirits.

In her mind at that very moment, Azúcar heard with undiluted clarity the ancient chant of her long departed grandmother, *doña* Fela, cry out…"*Lwa mwen, aprè Papa Ogou, m' se sou kont ou* [My spirits, after Papa Ogou, I am In your hands]."

Don Anselmo was certain that he too had heard his deceased comrade's familiar chant. Now kneeling, both supplicants turned their eyes upward to the front wall in the room whereupon hung two elegant, beautifully crafted sequined *'drapo'* [flags]: one bearing the magnificently beautiful image of Mayanèt, the other with the likeness of a smiling Ezili Dantò--those two notoriously powerful ladies. With eyes closed tightly, the former *batey* elder prayed hard that his suspicions about the true identity of Nelson Campos de la Rosa would be proven completely wrong *"Por el amor de todo lo sagrado"* [For the love of everything sacred]. Tell me, Oh Angels from underneath the waters, that those evil horrors from our shared past have not resurfaced--for whatever reasons-- only to bring undeserved misfortune and misery upon our young innocents; they should not be sacrificed as the targets of some undeserved vengeance; please do not allow this to happen. Let nothing but good be placed in the paths of these of these two extraordinary young individuals with such a brilliant future ahead of them. Please reveal to me in what manner have Mayanèt and her companion Ezili Dantò been offended so that we can straighten things out."

It was Azúcar's turn. Her supplication was equally genuine and agonizing. "*Ay, por el amor de mi sagrada abuelita* [For the love of my sacred grandmother]." Her voice was quivering as she held back her tears of affliction ... a dilemma of mixed sentiments. "*Mi sancta abuelita* [My sainted grandmother, I want nothing but pure joy and continuous success for my precious daughter, and also for her young friend. Yet, I feel the pain in my tortured heart that there is something not right about this relationship between my Alegrita and her friend Nelson. There is something that discomforts me and makes me feel afraid. '*Por favor, abuelita*', please reveal to me what it is that causes so much anxiety in my heart; what is it that churns my insides when *mi princesa* says how captivated she is by this young man's very presence? *Abuelita*, I beg you now with purity of heart, please reveal to me who Nelson Campos de la Rosa really is."

After a few short minutes had passed, an uninvited zephyr suddenly entered the sacred space of the altar room; the gentle breeze moved upward slowly to the '*drapo*' hanging on the front wall. The two flags fluttered quietly as the breeze seized hold firmly of the edges of both flags. Ezili Dantò seemed to smile more broadly, and Mayanèt ... approvingly.

"*Dlo kler va koule devan ou* "[Clear water will flow in front of you]," a hushed, comforting voice whispered. That voice was neither that of the old man nor that of his younger friend who had gone into the alter room with him to pray; unmistakably, they both heard the same whispered message. The two individuals glanced at each other in mutual comprehension. The three candles that *don* Anselmo had lighted earlier upon entering the room were still burning determinedly. According to ritual, he extinguished the flame of each candle. Now with absolute satisfaction, the two long-time friends from the old *batey* left the sacred room ... neither of them uttering a single word; it wasn't necessary.

DOCE

Back at her university in Colorado, Alegra was ecstatic upon receiving official word that she had been selected to become part of a skilled team of young climate science climate science students that would accompany several world renowned experts within the climatology community on a three-month expedition to the Caribbean. The scholarly project would involve a wide range of in-depth investigations of the ongoing, as well as the long-range effects of recently recorded manifestations of climate change occurring in the Caribbean region. The prestigious investigation team was being funded by a grant from an international research foundation. Alegra, because of her demonstrated stellar academic performance as a student concentrating in the area of climate science, had previously been the recipient of a similar opportunity that took her to Africa's Sahel zone and also to Somalia to study the desertification in those particular regions. When she shared the exciting news with Nelson, he was enormously proud of his sweetheart's achievement; his happiness was overwhelming.

"Mi querida flor [My dear flower], how awesome!" he yelled joyously. "This is our chance to return home together and be able to announce officially our relationship to our families. Won't they be surprised! We'll all celebrate together."

Without hesitating for a second, Nelson decided that he would interrupt temporarily his own studies in order to be with Alegra on this important trip. There was also the thrilling revelation that the selected site for the investigations was their own little *Isla.* Could the ancient Island spirits have been more generous in presenting the elated couple with a more divine gift? Of course, though, these modern young science students would know nothing about that.

"*Pero, mi precioso amor* [But, my precious love]," Alegra responded with surprise. "What might your parents say if you take that amount of time away from your studies? Remember, *mi amor*, you're on special scholarship. And what about those upcoming championship matches? The team is depending heavily on you as their captain. You know how important the tournament is."

"Alegrita, in all honesty, nothing ...absolutely *nada* is more important to me than being with you, especially right now, wherever you are. As for my parents --and God knows how much I love and respect them--- when they see how much in love I am with you, they'll totally understand and approve of my actions. And as far as the *fútbol* [soccer] team is concerned, those guys are extremely good and capable of winning that championship without me. That trophy is ours. Don't you see that this trip home together is really part of our shared fate '*No te confías en el nuestro destino?'* [Don't you trust our Destiny?] I can only imagine what's waiting for us back home ... your delicious '*pastelillos'*, for one thing." Nelson laughed teasingly.

As the pair made preparations for their anticipated trip back home, Alegra's mother was also preparing herself emotionally for her daughter's long-awaited homecoming of her *princesa.* Azúcar, however, agonized intensively about Alegra's return to the *Isla.* On the one hand, there was a mother's natural pride in a daughter's extraordinary academic accomplishments and personal development in every regard. But at the same time, there was that same mother's embedded sense of instinctive protectiveness that was supposed to prevent the young girl's precipitous plunge into dangerous, possibly injurious waters.

For the mother, her little girl's falling in love with Nelson Campos de la Rosa was certain to be one such perilous descent.

"*Por mi santísima abuelita* [For the sake of my most saintly grandmother], my innocent *princesa* has no earthly idea of exactly who this Nelson Campos de la Rosa is. But *abuelita* has revealed his identity to me. *Ay, díos mío.* This relationship was doomed from the start; it should never have happened in the first place. How do I tell her without risking what she believes in her heart is her true happiness? How will she understand?"

For however clearly the waters recently flowed before this distraught mother after visiting Mamá Lola's sacred altar room with old *don* Anselmo, Azúcar was nevertheless now facing an oppressive dilemma as only a mother in dire agony could. So therefore, Alegra's return trip home after being away for almost three long years of exciting and rewarding study and learning about the world was to be a complicated mix of surprises for everybody. In *don* Anselmo's case, while he too was awaiting Alegra's return with exuberance, the *'viejo sabio'* harbored a recognizable angst about the viability of the relationship that has now crescendoed into a fully blossomed romance between the young couple. The old wise man's suspicions-- as always -- have now been made unequivocally clear upon that mandatory visit to the altar room with his friend that day.

"*Bay kou bliye, pot mak sonje*," he said aloud, being reminded, of course, that the traditional Kreyòl proverb meant... 'Those who give out the blows forget, while those who bear the scars remembers well.'"

He also remembered something else that he used to hear while working as a young cane cutter... "Mayanèt is not always sweet; she can often be a tough and vengeful spirit." The old man wondered exactly how he was going to navigate the delicate terrain of truth, while at the same time avoiding the accompanying pain and perhaps remorse in the pending dilemma... especially involving someone he loved so very dearly.

'La famni sanble'... The family is assembled. That's the way *don* Anselmo always used to announce to the folks called together during times of crisis in the *batey*; it was made clear that an important meeting was about to start. Of course, in those days so long past, everybody automatically constituted *'family'* and the particular crisis was usually one that affected the entire community. The announcement was the traditional

way of dealing collectively with a vital issue or concern as determined by the revered council of elders. It was because of this long-honored practice, therefore, that Alegra's mother insisted urgently upon having her '*familia*' come together now on this very auspicious occasion.

For Azúcar, the event called for the combined protection and grace of all the ancestral spirits, as well as her personal will. *Don* Anselmo also felt it necessary to offer sweetest homecoming wishes to Alegra, and at the same time to offer the change for '*la famni*' to meet the young scholar's young sweetheart, Nelson Campos de la Rosa.

The old man could hear his honored comrade *doña* Fela-- now having made that hallowed journey to '*an ba dlo*'– utter in the clearest voice, "*la hierba mala que nunca muere...* weeds that never die."

With much frequency, she would remind everybody that ..."despite how hard you try to get rid of these ugly, useless annoyances, in time they still manage to reappear; they just keep coming back, They are impossible to kill."

And that is exactly how Azúcar eventually came to realize the sickness of the Island itself... this '*maldita isla* [this cursed island], as her grandmother always called it. So deeply rooted in the psyche is this infirmity that complete eradication becomes a self-delusionary lie. Many years ago, both Marcelo and Harold, the early committed mentors of a young, very bright little girl with the unusual skin color, living in the squalor of the *batey*, carefully navigated the girl's path to future university studies in Toronto. They had clearly expressed their sentiment about '*la hierba mala*' in terms of sugar. They witnessed first- hand what sugar had done to their beloved *Isla...* since the historical introduction and swift evolution of the sugar industry.

Moreover, there was an inevitably parallel development of monstrously brutal forms of plantation slavery and the oppression that ultimately led to physical, social and psychological death… all solely due to sugar. Azúcar's dedicated mentors had become thoroughly convinced that '*la hierba mala*' resulted in all the most grotesque manifestations of human degradation and exploitation across the *Isla*. For these two sensitive young mentors, this had been the conclusive argument … the morbid illusion of existence… that led the wise old Fela finally to allow Marcelo and Harold to take the young girl with them to Canada for a brilliant new life of stunning progress, enlightenment, and refinement.

So now, many many years after that initial traumatic departure, that same '*hierba mala*' would resurface in a horrendously deceptive form… a romantic liaison that both Azúcar and *don* Anselmo thought was not destined to be. This was how confirmed. The star-crossed young lovers represented but one more sorrowful instance of the unique malady afflicting the psyche of this otherwise idyllic Caribbean Eden. Seemingly disparate elements had been wove together by an inextricable fate… a fate no doubt that the ancient spirits themselves had confirmed. According to old *don* Anselmo, Mayanèt and Ezili Dantò were conspiring purposely to show that '*la hierba mala nunca muere.*'

TRECE

La Morenita Estate was easily overflowing with love, excitement, and genuine celebration for the return of the *princesa* after her long absence away from the *Isla*. Her success in Canada had been the topic of conversation since she completed her first year at the university. The joy could not be measured. Without exaggeration, she glowed radiantly and was effervescent in every sense; she was happy to be home. With equal enthusiasm and delight, she at last had the chance to introduce Nelson to her mother and to the 'assembled family.'

..."This has to be the happiest day of my life," she said with shameless giddiness. "I can't believe that both Nelson and I are actually standing here together in the same house where I grew up." After all those many lengthy telephone chats, and numerous emails and texted messages to her mother about Nelson, Alegra finally would learn forthrightly her mother's true and unfiltered thoughts regarding the young man who had become the unobstructed focus of her heart and of her secret dreams.

Marie Chauvet, Azúcar's *'hermana del alma'* [soul sister], and uncompromising promoter of the *Isla's* traditional culture, was present. "I could never have missed this occasion for any reason," she said smilingly. Since adolescence, Marie's grandmother had convinced her that the sacred spirits had chosen the extraordinarily talented young girl as the preferred *'mount'* of the *lwa* Papa Guidé. Little Marie didn't understand at first; she was frightened by the idea of a 'mounting' -- occurring during a spiritual trance when an individual becomes 'possessed' by a particular *lwa* and thus is said to be 'mounted' or 'entered.' It had been Marie's grandmother who revealed to this gifted child many of the obscure mysteries and secrets of the *Isla's* sacred traditions before the family decided that the girl should be sent away to Canada to live and be thoroughly educated about the broader world outside the *Isla*. It was therefore no coincidence that Marie Chauvet's early history was in many ways almost parallel with that of her childhood friend Azúcar. On this momentous evening in Alegra's honor, Marie made a remark that evoked those days of her grandmother's tutoring. *"Sak vide pa kanpe"*... 'An empty sack cannot stand up.

"How true that is, *mi querida hermana* [my dear sister]", Azúcar replied. *"Mi abuelita* always felt the same way. She used to say exactly that about our spiritual selves and how much we all need that special support."

Marie Chauvet assured everybody, "This will be an extremely memorable homecoming for our Alegrita."

Present also were Chelaine and Silvio Roumain, and like Marie Chauvet, among Azúcar's most cherished and trusted confidants over the years. They too shared many memoriesfrom the past. These two special individuals were highly respected social icons throughout the *Isla* for their long-time commitment to social and political justice. Both also felt it a binding obligation to be present at this important event for spiritual support to their friend Azúcar. It wasn't far into the balmy evening when Silvio stepped out onto the veranda of *La Morenita* and reflected upon a similar evening many years ago in the *batey* when he had been invited to a private meeting one night with *don* Anselmo at the elder's cabin. Silvio recalled with sweet nostalgia the conversation between the two men – one man burning with youthful, justifiable, yet impatient rage; the other, a resolute and measured elder offering insightful wisdom and many years of rich experiences gained from a long life dictated solely by the brutal sugarcane culture

"Escúchame bien, mi hijo. Hear me well, my son. It is now time to restore your spirit and redeem the soul of your sacred ancestors. You are a powerful *'kòk kalite'* [fighting rooster], without realizing it. This red rooster is sacred to Ogou, our

invincible warrior spirit. I give you this *kòk kalite* for protection; it will help you navigate successfully the difficult road that lies ahead of you. It will place itself at the magic crossroad so that you will be armed with fighting, but thoughtful toughness."

Silvio never forgot *don* Anselmo's instructive counsel; it helped build the core of Silvio's beliefs that the young warrior would carry with him along the various paths throughout his activist life. He turned to his wife Chelaine and said, "I am solidly convinced that even with all the hurtful inequities and suffering of every dimension, there are nevertheless many things anointed with unquestioned truths and real meaning." Therefore, for him, upon this occasion of Alegra's homecoming, Ogou's fighting rooster would again be needed to ward off the onslaught of *'la hierba mala.'*

For Chelaine, this celebratory evening secretly recalled her own inauspicious return to the *Isla* many years before. Sadly, Chelaine was still haunted by the specter of her demonic and reprehensible father, Mario Montalvo. Long ago, both she and her twin sister Cécile decided purposely to discontinue and abandon altogether the use of what they regarded 'the shameful Montalvo surname', replacing it with the 'far more prestigious and distinguished' Desgraves name of their maternal grandparents. Chelaine's urgent concern for the brilliant, but innocent young couple was that "these blissful lovers are unwittingly entangled in a very complicated and agonizing circumstance that is certain to result in ominous consequences for both young students

"I remember how at first nearly everybody felt that the union between you and Silvio was heading toward unavoidable catastrophe," Azúcar said to Chelaine. "Now in this moment, very similar feelings about the consequences of two young people who seem to be deeply in love with each other are indeed troubling, even frightening because of what we've learned about this young man, Nelson Campos de la Rosa."

Cécile and her husband Tomás Polanco, Jr. were equally concerned about providing their dear friend Azúcar the emotional girder that they felt she needed tonight in this uncertain situation. They were also certain that Alegra herself would soon learn about the far from coincidental thread woven so neatly through the relationship among this assembled *'famni'*. Moreover, Cécile used the evening's celebration to think about her own discomforting return to the *Isla* many years earlier. At the same time, that return ended what had been a forced exile for an anxious young couple helplessly in love; they had wanted merely to avoid the explosive anger and hostility of her family. The name 'Montalvo' had always personified "wrathful hatred, malice, and ruthlessness."

In her husband's case, the Polancos were the exact opposite ... humble and loving folk in regard. They had come from a long line of historically exploited sugarcane workers who had known nothing else but *la hierba mala* since the first Polanco's arrival at *Esperanza Dulce* plantation. Tomás, Jr.'s entire family believed with uninhibited honesty that... *'amor con amor se paga'* [love begets love]. Throughout their lives they all operated with this single belief.

"We have always lived by this code since the time of our *'abuelos'* [grandparents]," Tomás, Jr. said. "And I have accepted this belief without question," he assured his wife.

Theirs was a compelling story. The Montalvo daughter and her emboldened young cane cutter eloped and spent most of their married life together as a politically transformed couple in Revolutionary Cuba. As a result, Cécile became nearly always in perfect synchronization with her highly enlightened and more socially conscious husband. They both shared an identical ideological transformation upon learning about a much broader, more humane world with purpose. Now, after many years of learning so much about life itself, the two ex-patriots were strangely witnessing the same anxieties they had experienced upon their own uncertain return to the Isla as young Alegra and Nelson on this occasion... again, more than mere coincidence.

Of course, the evening would not have been complete without the presence of the much admired and devoted couple Marcelo and Harold. The unique bond formed and cemented between Alegra's mother and the two exceptionally courageous gentlemen was so enduring that it was inconceivable that they not be present. Marcelo and Harold had long ago survived the community's derision and vile personal assaults directed against them because of their controversial same-sex union. It was true that Marcelo and also Harold were once regarded as pariahs within the local society... however hypocritical this society was. Among the Montalvo brothers, Marcelo was the youngest, the most educated, the most sophisticated and refined. Without fail, everybody always remarked, "He is the most gentle and sweetest human being you'd ever want to know." But this same community was intolerant when it came to the question of "two men living together like husband and wife. *Que vulgaridad*! What vulgarity!"

Dr. Harold Capps, Marcelo's life partner, was a twenty-seven year old Canadian agronomist when he first arrived on the *Isla*. His considerable expertise in global sugarcane cultivation had earned him distinction, and so the multinational corporate headquarters in Toronto assigned the brilliant agronomist to the *Isa*. His mission was to conduct extensive investigations into the probable causes of the corporation's declining sugarcane harvest yields. Capps arrived prepared to investigate various questions related to cane stalk density, rainfall averages, soil conditions insect infestations, fertilizers and the like. However, the young scientist found absolutely nothing that would explain what was happening to the corporation's sugarcane interests.

Instead, it was the *'viejo sabio' don* Anselmo who actually made the 'discovery'; unselfishly and rather thoughtfully, the old man passed his findings to the 'Sugar Doctor-- as Capps became widely known. The answer had been found in the form of the legendary *chotacabra* bird. The *batey*'s old wise man had long noticed that a recent influx of these dread, mysterious birds had begun nesting in an abandoned section of the cane fields, bringing with them a heretofore unfamiliar and undetected parasite. It was this extremely harmful parasite that was causing the unexpected rapid deterioration in the cane crop.

In time, the two young men, very much in love with each other, quite brazenly defied local convention and set up housekeeping together. Over the years, they forged a meaningful bond of mentorship, loyal friendship and unconditional love with young Azúcar and soon after with here revered grandmother *doña* Fela, with Lucien and then with the little *princesa*, upon her birth. It was Marcelo and Harold who very meticulously engineered the remarkable metamorphosis in Azúcar's amazing life. She was thus able to escape, of course, with her grandmother's blessings-- the otherwise certain doom of awaiting her if she had remained trapped on *la isla.*

"Mi querida azúcar morenita," my darling little lump of brown sugar, remember that *la hierba mala nunca muere,"* a moribund *doña* Fela found the strength to whisper to her tearful lump of brown sugar before departing to *'an da dlo'.* Wipe away your tears and don't be afraid. Leave this misery; If you stay, *'la hierba mala'* will destroy you just as it has destroyed all of us. *'La maldita caña'* is the true and certain enemy here. In every ounce of its cursed sweetness, it will bring you down. Go now, *'mi hijita'*, before it's too late."

So, the innocent, confused young girl left the Island with her two mentors to begin a new and frightfully challenging life far removed from *'la hierba mala'*. "Oh Angels in the water, may the ancestral spirits protect you always," said the woman upon closing her eyes for the last time

CATORCE

For all those genuinely compassionate, individuals, all of course with their own gripping personal stories, all forming '*la famni sanble*', all now in attendance to share the joy of Alegra's homecoming, each remembered with incalculable chaffing the horrific cycle of Montalvo madness and viciousness. From their individual perspective, they all were certain that the cycle had come to a bittersweet end with the demise of the brothers Miguel and Manolo -- suffering the same grotesque fate as had the older sibling Mario much earlier. They all remembered quite well; but this otherwise jubilant gathering proved far from having finally ended. This anxiously awaited evening would be simply the precursor for a slow descent before spiraling further downward into a continuous acceleration toward recognizable desolation and inevitable ruin. All the individual who had assembled together were unprepared for this plunge. True, *don* Anselmo, like all the other guests, was extremely happy and eager for Alegra's return; but he concealed tremendous misgivings and uneasiness about this evening. With certainty, he knew that before the night ended, he along with everyone else would have to commit to naked honesty in revealing what they each felt about the meaning of any possible romantic union between their Alegrita and her fellow classmate, compatriot and professed sweetheart, Nelson Campos de la Rosa

The evening was enviably radiant... glorious in every sense. The enchanting sounds of the evening, more than anything else, were most notable. Birds, not yet ready for their customary and timely sleep, chattered high in the trees. The early evening light ushered in a trail of harmless, typically sweet Caribbean sounds-- screeching vervet monkeys, chirping, tiny tree frogs and jittery crickets, shrilling cuckoos, bellowing bullfrogs, crying doves-- if indeed they were crying at all. The collection of sounds, of course, would come to an abrupt halt by the light of dawn, which was still far away. However, everyone present to honor Alegra noticed an immediate difference--- *la sequía* caused the customarily large yellow and red blooms of the frangipani bushes to no longer emit the seductive perfume across the evening air. The always- present delicacy of the night breezes no longer whispered through the silk-cotton trees-- now completely dried up; so the soft leaves that would normally grace these trees weren't able to brush together. The *sequía* produced an absence of the once intoxicating aroma of a unique coalescence of flavors: sugar apple, orange, soursop, tamarind, *guanábana*. Again, '*la maldita sequía*' was successful in preventing an otherwise delicious tropical fruit punch concoction.

"*Peyi-ap fini nan lanmè.*" [The country is going to end up in the sea]," *don* Anselmo usually whispered to himself whenever he viewed a given situation with exasperation. His patience was running short after countless warnings and ominous predictions. "*Coño!* How many damn times do I have to keep saying the same thing?" Even so, the evening was a special joy for everyone who had come together to receive both Alegra and her declared sweetheart Nelson.

Much thought went into planning the meal for this exceptional evening ... an exquisite meal designed to please Alegra after having been absent for so long. Azúcar knew that only the household cook Ambrosia could prepare such a meal that everyone would receive with unwavering satisfaction. Ambrosia had arrived at *La Morenita* as a young, untested assistant to Mamá Lola years ago and learned the many tedious step-by-step procedures of food preparation from the legendary '*reina*' [queen] of Island culinary arts. Mamá Lola had been employed with the Origène-Desgraves household for many years prior. The meal was sumptuously Caribbean fare -- everything that Mamá Lola knew would please the gastronomic desires of the diners, but most especially Alegra: broiled dolphin in white wine and Portobello garlic sauce, codfish cakes, shrimp crêpes, pumpkin soup, baked cassava rolls with a tasty sautéed beef filling, an entrée consisting of a slow-cooking *'pernil a la parilla'* [suckling pig roasted over a traditional outdoor stone pit], with herb and olive stuffing, roast lamb drenched in exotic condiments like mango and papaya chutneys, tropical ackee soufflé with green chiles and sweet onions.

Over the years as chief cook at *La Morenita*, Ambrosia had perfected an array of her unrivaled breads and sweet rolls that were eagerly sought after and currently still in demand at the most popular *'panadería'* [bakery] in town: coconut bread, and banana date-nut bread, among other original varieties. Of course, though, Mamá Lola alone assumed the task of preparing Alegra's favorite *'pastelillos'* that always used to be waiting for her upon her return from school every afternoon. Ambrosia also prepared Alegra's favorite desserts: guava pie and Caribbean rum raisin cake.

"A more seductive banquet table could not have been prepared for the *Isla's* ancestral gods, "someone was heard remarking in total seriously." *Felicidades y bienvenida de nuevo a nuestra querida Alegrita*! Congratulations and welcome back again to our dear Alegrita! Tonight is yours to savor; tonight we gather here to celebrate your extraordinary success in your academic pursuits, but more than anything else your anxiously awaited return to us," Marcelo said as he initiated the successive rounds of the evening's toasts. He raised his champagne glass high and blew a loving kiss in the honoree's direction, then blew another kiss to the proud mother standing alongside Alegra. After each of the other 'family members' poured forth with their individual *'saludos', 'felicidades,' 'que viva nuestra Alegrita' 'con mucho amor'*, [cheers, m congratulations, with much love, long live our dearest Alegra]-- all for a visibly elated Alegra.

It now became Nelson's moment to step forward in raising his glass in his sweetheart's honor. The young man had already been properly introduced earlier in the evening upon his arrival, and everyone was very gracious towards Alegra's special guest. However, as anticipated, there was the natural curiosity and muted speculation about Nelson that had circulated prior to his arrival. For the most part, everyone in attendance knew something about the strange twist of fate involving young Nelson's familial relationship with certain members of the community. But there were none of the awkward stares nor any signs of scorn or disdain. To the contrary, all the comments were whimsical and genuinely innocent.

"*Qué guapo es.* How very handsome he is," Marcus whispered into Harold's ear.

"He's a real cuttie," Harold agreed.

"I think it's uncanny how much he resembles all the Montalvo men," Marie Chauvet observed.

Chelaine thought that the young man was extremely traditional, even old-fashioned, in his manner. Nelson's toast began, "*A mi querida amor.* To my dearest darling. I offer you my humble heart that has been conquered by your precious love and by your sincere desire for our long happiness together." Even with everyone automatically raising their glass in reponse to Nelson's surprising toast, only Azúcar and *don* Anselmo directed their immediate gaze at each other. Were they registering their uneasiness about the evening? Perhaps they were preparing themselves for the inevitable plunge? The two said nothing; their nervous eyes merely locked together in a mutually perceptive agreement. All the other guests also instinctively sensed the beginning of the descent. Sadly, though, the starry-eyed young lovers remained clueless.

The toasts ended and the splendid meal was served after everyone was seated around the huge, ornate, hand-crafted native *ceiba*-wood dining table; this was an heirloom that

Yvette Origène-Desgraves had presented to Azúcar and Lucien as a wedding gift. As with most dinner parties everywhere throughout the *Isla* in recent months, table conversation here also inevitably shifted anxiously to the topic foremost on everyone's mind-- the noticeably advancing *sequía* currently devastating the landscape. Immediately following comments and questions about Alegra's impressive academic triumphs abroad, idle talk about Nelson's championship soccer matches and much deserved accolades, overall university life, the singularly urgent concern turned to the drought. Nobody as yet broached the specifics of Nelson's parentage or any attempts to probe deeper into the young man's life generally. As everyone knew, because both Alegra and Nelson were aspiring climatologists and could eagerly offer a wealth of informed comment and explanation about global warming, all attention centered upon the two brilliant university science students.

First, Alegra shared with the gathering her recent, unique experience with an world-renown team of professors and selected students who had traveled to the African continent in order to study critical drought conditions in that part of the world. Then, Nelson told his attentive audience about the remarkable opportunity presently being afforded his sweetheart to participate in investigations of observable climate change taking place in the Caribbean; in fact, their own native *Isla* was to be the base for project operations. Nelson, as everybody learned, made the decision to accompany the research team even though he was not participating officially in the multitude of scholarly tasks involved. The mere idea of returning home together could not have motivated him more.

"*Ay, que bueno.* How wonderful. It would be a chance for us to meet each other's family. I couldn't have wished for a sweeter dream come true." Nelson grinned broadly as he glanced toward Alegra, who returned a loving smile of approval. Azúcar, as well as the others, was eager to learn as much as possible about the precise nature of what sounded like a dynamic research project and one in which her *princesa* was truly fortunate in being able to participate.

"*Mi querida hijita*, your father would be so proud of you, and most certainly your *'bisabuela Fela'* [great-grandmother Fela]."

Alegra began by acknowledging the alarming obstacles that, in large measure, have plagued the team's efforts throughout their studies, making even more difficult any strongly convincing arguments. She mentioned, for instance, how very unfortunate and sometimes discouraging it had been for so many individuals --many of them otherwise intelligent people who should really know better-- to simply mock and sneer dismissively at the notion of climate change and global warming. Meanwhile, the last two previous decades have confirmed other earlier findings -- establishing clearly that human activity is directly related to the melting of the Arctic ice caps, the collapse of worldwide fish stocks and the rapid rates of extinction within all classes of life forms. It ceases to be just speculation. It is a proven fact, but so many people seem to ignore these facts.

There was urgency in her voice. Nelson added as if on cue, "And we see this as a matter of the extinction of much of what sustains life forms such as ourselves. Imagine that, if you can." Accordingly, Nelson made the point that there is so much evidence, substantiated by hard evidence contained in many scientific reports, to suggest that unless something is done really fast, the air quality will continue to deteriorate, temperature will steadily rise, and oceans will become too acidic even to support their present diversity.

That was the principle reason that the university's research group was coming down to the region; there is no question that the Caribbean is one of the planet's most bio-diverse regions in every regard. Historically, the Caribbean has presented this formidable challenge... and continues to do so. Alegra felt proud of Nelson's accurate presentation, especially-- as everyone knew-- he was not an officially designated member of the investigating team. He was nevertheless amazingly attentive and alert as a climate science student himself.

Harold, the former 'Sugar Doctor', was quick to offer solid confirmation of what Nelson had just said. "I suggest we consider what's already happened in the United States and across Europe. Wheat, corn, and soybean production is at record low yields. Very frightening. For the past two years, these crops have almost been ruined totally, naturally resulting in unbelievably high food prices everywhere ... even in the wealthier nations. Right here in every corner of the *Isla*, we see that food prices have more than doubled."

Marie Chauvet had recently returned to the Caribbean after a lengthy stay in Southern France and while there became astutely aware of the dramatically transformed landscape in that European region.

"There was a maddening concern about French champagne production. According to everybody I talked with, the entire region was heavily impacted; production was the lowest in about forty years because of the drought crisis spreading all across Europe. So, it should come as no surprise that high global emissions producing harmful greenhouse gases are extremely high. This situation is undoubtedly the cause of what we are witnessing right now as global warming."

"*Se lé koulév mouri, ou konn longé longé lá* [Only after the serpent is dead can you take its measure]", *don* Anselmo began in his forceful voice, despite his advanced years. No one was ever certain of the old man's exact age. It had also been the same way with his noble comrade *doña* Fela, even at the moment of her death. '*El viejo sabio*' listened silently, patiently, and cautiously to every remark made by conscientious souls throughout the evening. He pondered carefully the ramifications of each person's comments before considering his own broader, most collective and more encompassing response before addressing '*La famni sanble*'. It was exactly as it had been so many years ago in the case with the Sugar Doctor's painfully exhaustive efforts at the time in attempting to find credible explanations for the devastatingly low sugarcane harvest yields. The former old sage of the *batey* now arrived at what was --at least in line with his own prudence--- the only acceptable reason for this current drought crisis. Upon careful deliberation, the old man was ready at last to share with '*la famni*' those disturbing thoughts.

QUINCE

"*Coño!* I don't know if my old worn-out heart will ever know happiness again. My soul is now like that of my sacred African ancestors longing for the comforting evening shadows once they landed against their will as deceived and helpless captives upon these hostile Caribbean shores--- as deceived and helpless captives. Life eventually withers more quickly than the cane fields and wild grasses. This has always been the destiny of all those who forget or who ignore the sacred spirits... so perishes the hope of the godless. And now what we are seeing is a drying up of all living things because of our foolish betrayal of the ancestors.

'*Tout komplis nan mizè nou.*'[All of us are complicit in our misery.] In one way of another, at some time or other, we all have disobeyed the spirits. And dammit, we continue to do so even with all the warnings we've received. For that, we are paying a heavy price in the form of this '*maldita sequía*' ... that is what's causing everything, including our very souls to wither away. We have been disrespectful."

The old man had not finished. "I can still remember when I was a young boy cutting cane alongside the *batey* elders; they were constantly warning us--- especially if the community had foolishly disrespected the gods. Our elders would say, '*If the gods hold back the waters, there will be certain drought; if they let the waters loose, those waters will devastate the land.*' To the sacred spirits belong strength and victory. *Ou ka konprann mwen?* You can understand me, can't you?"

What shot forth next from the angry old man's mouth was much more than empty babble-- even though there was an unconscious weaving of traditional Island Kreyol, vernacular Spanish and English. He had previously directed his collections to all the assembled guests. Everyone was still very attention, clinging to the man's every word. Hesitating for a few seconds before continuing, he changed his tone to more directly focus on both Alegra and Nelson. The true surprise was that nobody except the young lovers registered shock or disbelief at what *don* Anselmo said next. His penetrating gaze was unflinching as it landed squarely upon the two young students for whom everything said earlier had been intended.

Candid and straightforward described the *'viejo sabio's'* message. But at the same time, his message was neither brusque nor offensive; that would have been unlike him under any circumstances. He always said exactly and clearly what he meant in order to convey without the slightest desire of taking a circuitous path in coming to his central point.

"*Escúchanme bien* [Hear me well]. For all that is sacred, you two young people must not ... cannot continue this romance. It is futile; it is the will of the sacred spirits that you do not continue this thing --- this love you say you have for each other. No matter how much you may *think* it is true love, it is like this dreaded *sequía*. It brings nothing but ultimate doom, nothing but dryness and a prolonged absence of fruitfulness. It will do unimagined harm and cause destructive ugliness along every inch of its path. That is what lies ahead of you both. *'Ou ka konprann mwed?'*"

Marcelo quickly intervened in order to translate the traditional expression for the stunned couple, suspecting, however, that Nelson did indeed understand. Alegra turned toward her mother, who was now standing at her daughter's side for emotional support.

"*Por el amor de mi santísima abuela*. For the love of my sainted grandmother," Azúcar begged of her daughter, who was exposed emotionally and was visibly shaken by what she and everyone else had just heard from *don* Anselmo.

"Believe me, *mi princesa*," Azúcar tried to explain. "It hurts my heart to the core to have you hear this truth; but *don*

Anselmo is absolutely right. It's exactly what your beloved great- grandmother Fela would say if she were here with us right now. Both you and Nelson must listen very carefully and understand what is being said to you. *Don* Anselmo as our respected elder has always been the conveyer of nothing but pure truth precisely because our ancestral spirits speak to him directly; it has always been so."

"*Mi querida hijita,* I know you never really accepted most, if any of our traditions. Our old ways have seemed strange or maybe even a little foolish to you; we all knew that. I'm sure you always thought that many of our traditions were just ignorant superstitions, constantly competing against your modern science for your attention. But *'mi cielo'* [my dearest], we always knew that these sacred traditions were no match for your growing appetite for science. The will of both Mayanèt Ezili Dantó is far more powerful than all the science and technology that you and Nelson could ever learn in a hundred years sitting in your university classrooms and laboratories. These two very dynamic spirits together can be extremely vengeful, but also protective and loving. You and Nelson can do nothing but accept what we're telling you. You two have no idea how much past horror surrounds and infiltrates your relationship; there is so much cursed history involved in all this."

Azúcar's motherly face was drenched in tears. The consequences of the shocking 'revelation' about Nelson Campos de la Rosa were like those of the reality of climate change ... a reality that could not be denied under any possibly circumstances. Sadly, those circumstances had the disastrous effects of huge, irresponsible amounts of carbon emissions into the atmosphere. Mother and daughter alike immediately felt the shock of the revelation. Caught next in the fast moving avalanche of elusive, baffling emissions was Nelson himself. Receiving no prior warning of any kind, he was jolted by everything that he had just heard. He didn't even know where to begin as he sifted through all this confusing new information. He remembered hearing, however, something that *don* Anselmo said more than once.

"*M'hijo*. My son, let your ears and your heart take in what I am saying, Very deliberate omission has shrouded the real truth. Everything, of course, happened so very long before either you or Alegrita was even born."

Marcelo thought to himself, "Now, the dilemma conflicting all the key players in this unfolding saga is just how to handle this revelation in a sensible and intelligent manner ... and without causing panic." Marcelo decided not to share this thought with even Harold. Marcelo decided not to share this thought with even Harold.

Again, for mother and daughter, as well as for Nelson and his family, but also for *don* Anselmo, the irritating question centered around whether each one separately or all of them collectively as essential players would proceed beyond the pending spiral to what irrefutably was a doomed romance from the start for the inexperienced lovers. The other path was whether the relationship, for however genuine the couple regarded it, should be halted altogether ... brought to a definitive end without any question. Period. The aftermath was guaranteed to produce distasteful results along either path... according all observers. Like the now raging *sequía*, Azúcar was left barren spiritually by what she ultimately learned about the true identity of her daughter's sweetheart.

Don Anselmo, whose initial suspicions and misgivings were not solidly confirmed, was tormented even more deeply than earlier. The despicable brutality that had plagued the Island's entire labor force so regularly in the past had returned at this present time and in this space. This return served to remind everybody of the frequently unpredictable and sometimes precarious actions of that powerful duo, Mayanèt and Ezili Dantò. But despite which would be the chosen path, the one focal element presenting the difficult challenge would be the uncompromising love that Alegra and Nelson held in their respective hearts.

"*Carajo!* How I used to torture myself every night for so many years as I pleaded with the ancestral spirits for a peaceful sleep... wanting desperately to know 'why'? '*Por qué?*' I often suspected as much because Mayanèt was rebuking us for what happened in the '*Bosque de Flores*' long ago that unforgettable day. Everybody suspected that the sacred spirits were never pure in the eyes of any of those Montalvos. As decadent and corrupt as they were – all of them except Marcelo, of course-- were monsters of men who drank up evil like it was sugared water!" *Don* Anselmo was describing the most repugnant scourge of the *batey*, Mario Montalvo.

"That monster was the most frightening thing during those dark times at *Esperanza Dulce;* he alone was responsible for so many of our woes."

The old man's still incredibly lucid memory transported the attentive listeners -- all of whom seemingly had fallen into a mesmerizing trance-- far back into the past to recount for both Alegra and Nelson the heinous event that took place in '*El Bosque de Flores.*'

"*Bay kou bliye, pot mak sonje* [Those who give out the blows forget, while those who bear the scars remember well]. I will never forget how it happened. A young cane cutter named Jèrôme Valcin was seeking revenge for the earlier killing of this beloved older brother Césaire.

As it happened, Césaire and his best friend happened to be returning to the *batey* after spending a night of merriment at a workers' settlement located some distance away. The two men, more than sufficiently inebriated, were totally unaware that they were being stalked; unknown armed individuals had followed every step of the two revelers on their way back to their own settlement. Completely without warning, the two friends were fatally shot down at close range like two helpless rabbits ... their limp bodies riddled with more bullet holes than anybody could count.

Miguel and Manolo Montalvo, as it was revealed, were the determined stalkers and culprits of this cowardly deed. They had been relentless in their avenging pursuit of the killer or killers of their older sibling a few years earlier. In their blind rage, they randomly accosted the first unsuspecting victims they stumbled without knowing with any degree of certainty—and really didn't care—the identity of the actual perpetrators of Mario's murder or innocence or guilt of the two cane cutters caught in the trap that particular day in the forest. Miguel and Manolo were like hungry wolves in search of raw meat and were aflame with a voracious appetite for retribution. Without any reservation or remorse, they assumed the simultaneous role of hunters, judges, and executioners.

The young Jérôme, whose presence that day in the '*Bosque*' was totally undetected by the pair of evil-willed stalkers, witnessed the killing of both his brother and his brother's companion. Thus, the youthful cutter vowed to avenge this killing, however long it would take to do so. A few years afterwards, the horribly mutilated bodies of Miguel Montalvo and his wife Gabriela were found hacked to pieces one deliciously balmy, dew-filled morning a few feet away from the winding path in the Flower Forest. The local authorities never apprehended the person or persons responsible for the hideous attack on the couple; young Jérôme was never suspected. The present 'revelation' was made clear during a recent visit that Azúcar and her old comrade *don* Anselmo made together to the sacred altar room at *La Morenita*.

"*Coño! Otra vez la maldita caña!* Dammit! Again, it's the goddamn sugarcane!" *Don* Anselmo concluded his riveting narrative. "Gabriela and Miguel Montalvo had two handsome sons; the first born they named Miguel, Jr. and a second... Nelson! Years later, both boys developed a remarkable athletic prowess, subsequently becoming two of the *Isla's* widely applauded *fútbol* [soccer] stars."

The bitter irony, though, was that Miguel was a younger brother to Mario Montalvo Marcelo, the youngest. As everybody knew at the time, it was Mario who had been the violent rapist of *doña* Fela's young granddaughter... now, of course, Alegra's mother. After so much reprehensible, seemingly endless vengeful bloodletting, all the surviving members of the Montalvo clan–again, with the single glorious exception of Marcelo-- made the rather sorrowful, but necessary decision to change the family name altogether; it became 'Campos de la Rosa'. Therefore, we now learn that Nelson Campos de la Rosa is an actual blood relation ... a nephew, in fact... to Marcelo Montalvo! Old *don* Anselmo did not hesitate to remind everybody, *"Kon sa bagay la yé* [That's the way it is here in the *batey.*]; it has always been like that]."

It became obvious to everybody who remembered that there was never a totally satisfactory explanation for what was considered 'the senseless reality' determining circumstances of the *batey* in those days. *'Kon sa bagay la yé* [That's the way it is here in the *batey*], is what *doña* Fela used to say. This present circumstance involving the two young science students became clear when Azúcar and *don* Anselmo made their recent visit together to the sacred altar room.

"I'm afraid there's something else the two of you should know," added Marcelo in his urgency to reveal as yet another dreadful misgiving about the relationship between Alegra and Nelson. *"Ay, por mi madre.* This is especially painful for me to have to remember even after all these years since the incident. Alegra, your mother would often tell us how she could never summon the courage to share with you so much of the ugliness and horror she experienced while living in that God-forsaken place with her beloved *abuelita doña* Fela. As much as she so wanted to do so, she felt that she simply couldn't. We all knew, however, that the right moment would eventually come when that terrible history would resurface. It's a history that can't -- nor shouldn't be hidden or denied under any circumstances, despite how painful it might be."

Thus began the unpleasant, but necessary and unavoidable narrative about one particular event from Azúcar's complicated past that had been deliberately kept secret from her little *princesa* for many years. Everybody in attendance for this special occasion hoped that the conclusive truth, finally, would be unveiled to the young couple so that they would realize *princesa* for many years. Everybody present at *La Morenita* for this special evening hoped that the conclusive truth, finally, would be revealed to the young couple so that they would realize for themselves and accept the futility of their relationship. The tension throughout the room was heavy and ominous. Alegra and Nelson together could feel the naked discomfort and therefore tried to clothe themselves for what was coming next.

Harold found Marcelo surprisingly blunt and straightforward, sparing nothing for the sake of revealing the truth. In visibly tortured detail, Marcelo described the shameful rape of a youthful, innocent virgin by his own older brother, the monster Mario. The heinous assault had sent unsettling ripples throughout the lives of everybody connected with *Esperanza Dulce* and far beyond. As Marcelo pointed out, the entire *batey* community seemed to accept the merciless consequences of that violent act with a kind of muffled anger in the same manner as they did with all the other horrors of their daily life in that space and time. The traumatized thirteen-year old victim was unmistaken in the identity of her depraved attacker, but as with every other aspect of the nightmarish circumstances of the *batey* in those days, Mario was never arrested or brought to justice. There had never been the slightest illusion of justice for residents of the *batey* communities. But there was a final piece of this narrative that contained parallel revulsion. It had to do with what happened after Azúcar gave birth to beautiful twin girls, the unforeseen result of Mario's savage violation of the young virgin. Far more painful consequences arrived soon afterwards.

Marcelo related to the sober listeners perhaps the worst part of Azúcar's truly sickening ordeal, the ancient tradition of the '*Marasa Bwa*' ritual. This was the practice, according to obscure tradition, muddled by considerable mystery, whereupon the elders concluded that it was a bad omen when twins-- normally regarded as sacred and in possession of certain magical powers bestowed by the sacred spirits-- had been born under 'evil' circumstances. It was said that "the mother was carrying a '*baka*' [evil spirit] inside her wound" and that Mario Montalvo's reprehensible act had offended deeply all the residents of the community. The *Marasa*] *Bwa* [Twins of the Forest] was a secretly performed ritual -- without witnesses— enacted by the most senior elders deep in the forest. It could only be correctly described, as both Marcelo and Harold remarked with unrestrained outrage at the time upon learning of this ceremony ... "*a hideous act of infanticide, equally as monstrous as was the rape itself ... symptomatic of the absolute decay of the maldito batey.*"

Even with all the reverence for the ancient traditions, Azúcar needed quite a period of time and distance to digest fully all that had happened in this regard. Her emotional pain was beyond measure. Given everything, the elders, especially *doña* Fela, had reminded the young girl that '*Jou va, jou vien, m'pa di passé ça.*' Everyboody was convinced that revenge would come eventually ... and when least expected; both Mayanèt and Ezili Dantò would guarantee it. Marcelo finished his jolting narrative before an absolutely solemn audience. Neither Alegra nor Nelson could find the strength to respond audibly; Alegra was weeping softly along with her mother, who remembered every detail as recounted so accurately by Marcelo. *Don* Anselmo broke the uneasy silence with his deliberate utterance. "*La mala hierba nunca muere.*"

Marcelo's narrative immediately produced nothing short of an avalanche of shattering reactions of unexpected proportions... enormously startling, horribly disturbing, painfully jarring to the senses. For both Alegra and Nelson, these descriptions were appropriate in attempting to explain the weight of all that had recently conspired to descend upon the young couple's individual psyches. The combined emotional toll, however, hadn't as yet been determined. Old *don* Anselmo used to always remind folks about such situations" *Se lé koulé mouri, ou konn longé li* [Only when the serpent is dead can you take its measure.]" Following lengthy and agonizing efforts to make the necessary connections of the seemingly disparate pieces of information recently brought to light, the confused young couple felt a sustained cold chill hover over them; it was as if that chill had penetrated their very souls.

"Wow!" Nelson struggled to summarize his immediate response... a simplistic, one-word utterance. *"Puede ser posible?"* Can this be possible?" he insisted of Alegra once the two of them were alone and had the chance to begin exploring together all that they had just heard. And a much needed exploration it was.

"I can't begin to tell you, *mi querida amor,* how I'll ever be able to process more clearly this mind-bogging, murky history that affects our future. I don't know how or where to begin sifting and sorting through all this."

The young science student and champion athlete was visibly shaken. At the same time, he was quite uneasy about the newly reveled events from a past so remote from his present circumstance. It was guaranteed that he would have serious difficulty trying to connect what appeared initially to be gnawing pieces of a gigantic puzzle designed purposely to jostle anybody's mind. Of course, Nelson had no clue about how to make all the pieces fit neatly together. Unfortunately, though, neither he nor his sweetheart had learned the important lessons of simply calling upon the *Isla'*s sacred ancestral spirits for help.

"It's absolutely amazing." Alegra responded. "No one ever mentioned any of this to me as I was growing up at *La Morenita.*

Mami, and surely not *Papi*, never seemed to want to share with me so much of their past lives, whether individually or jointly. They probably never had any intentions to ever do so ... always wanting, instead, to protect me from everything possible. But I do remember how Mamá Lola would often suggest to me that there were 'certain well-guarded '*secretos*' [secrets] in *Mami's* history that I would learn some day ... but not now because I wasn't ready.'"

"*Mi querida princesa*, I ask the sacred spirits to reveal to you other things in life just as fascinating to you as your science is ... and well before it's too late," Azúcar had said.

"Believe me, Nelson, I really didn't understand that last part of what *Tata abuelita* [my great-grandmother] had strongly emphasized. Alegra continued. "There was also my nanny Virgile; she was always try to teach me so much about the traditions and customs of our Isa; I suppose I just wasn't listening. I honestly didn't want to listen... especially if it wasn't related to science and world geography. Sometimes, I think about all those long afternoons after regular classes at the '*liceo*' when I was expected to be listening and absorbing volumes of important information — all those strange names and facts about sacred ancestral spirits, and so many confusing and outdated traditions and rituals. Poor Virgile, she really tried hard with me, but just wasn't able to compete with my deep love for science and technology."

For Nelson's part, after listening patiently and with pure compassion for his sweetheart, he was deliberate in his response. "But, *mi querida*, you do see what your Mamá Lola and Virgile were trying to prepare you for? It was for this very moment, right now. Don't you see how it all comes together? I admit that I myself am trying hard to see certain important connections."

It would be disingenuous to say that this revelation was not extremely troublesome for the two young lovers. These were two young university students, scientifically focused and astutely aware of the modern world around them -- but far removed psychologically and emotionally from their commonly-shared Caribbean *Isla* drenched in a long, turbulent ignorance. In the now-faded culture of the highly regimented and restrictive *batey* community, both *doña* Fela and *don* Anselmo, but also Mamá Lola, would easily had said that such a 'revelation' was far more than 'coincidence' since nobody believed that any particular event or occurrence was 'coincidental. Rather, unequivocally, as highly revered village elders, along with everybody else in the community, would have attributed any 'revelation' as ... "the expressed will of the sacred spirits; the gods had destined it so."

'*Jou va, jou vien, m' pa di passé ça* [Day comes, day goes; I'll say nothing more than that]. The cryptic tradition Kreyòl saying implies the speaker's superior grasp of the workings of a world-- especially the world of sugarcane-- where brutal injustices, inhumane exploitation, and unthinkable abuses used to occur daily, as perpetrated by the powerful against the powerless.

'*The days may come and go, but you just wait and see; my day is coming!*'

DIECISEIS

The agony that Alegra and Nelson were experiencing together... although perhaps not with equal intensity, was nevertheless quite similar to that which Alegra's mother herself had undergone many years earlier. More precisely, it was the difficulty of earnestly trying to navigate successfully or even with minimal effectively a world far removed from the narrowly restrictive ambiance of Caribbean sugarcane culture. It had been for Azúcar — for the young couple, as well, a world of overlapping appendages whereupon a person was expected to partake aggressively in the sophisticated, modern, and secular education buttressed with all the values and privileges accompanying that education outside those confines of Island society. At the same time, the individual found herself in the uncomfortable circumstance of a reluctant, unconscious hostage to the commanding beliefs and traditions of one's primary culture that had been left behind.

The experience is undoubtedly overwhelming, even for the strongest of individuals. With the current dilemma of exactly how to navigate this new terrain, the almost unbelievable 'revelation' presented to the young lovers required seeking wiser, more insightful advice. Only such counsel could come from '*los viejos sabios*', those respected community elders who many years ago had cast off all burdensome emotional baggage... thus rendering these wise and sober individuals totally free of any degree of bias in their counsel.

In Nelson's case, that advice came from his grandfather, who had lived in the same household with Nelson's family for as long as the young student could remember. The old man, much like so many other grandparents, tried many times in the past to share with all his grandchildren his treasured collection of personal stories about life in the *batey*. There were anecdotes of every kind, including those involving the old man's comrades *doña* Fela, *don* Anselmo, and Mamá Lola. But again like Alegra, Nelson simply was never genuinely interested in hearing about his grandfather's past. He preferred, instead, devoting the bulk of his energies and curiosity strictly to the 'mysteries of science,' and certainly not to the *Isla*'s sacred spirits' bearing strange-sounding names, or to remote ancestors, confusing traditions, and to what the younger generations labeled 'silly Island superstitions.'

"*Pero, abuelito*. But granddad, I'm really more excited about science and geography than I am about learning the names of all those so-called 'sacred spirits,'" Nelson once said innocently, but honesty to his grandfather, who was slightly offended by the boy's foolish remark. Nelson, of course, had nothing but absolute love and the highest respect for his '*abuelito*'; the entire community did. Nelson meant no offense whatsoever. By using the appropriateness of a traditional proverb of the *Isla*, the old man confidently reminded his rather naïve grandson of something very important.

"*Nunca hay nada nuevo debajo del sol ... y de noche todos los gatos son prietos* [There's nothing new under the sun ... and at night all cats are black.] I hope only that you won't allow your science to get in the way of acquiring meaningful wisdom-- a wisdom about those things that really matter in this life," the old man concluded with satisfaction.

But it was already too late. By not listening to what was meant as a clear warning and not paying attention to all the 'signs,' the young couple had made a grave mistake in deciding to become romantically linked ... "falling blindly in love," as someone said. It became obvious to everyone, perhaps more lucid to Marcelo, Nelson's uncle and to Azúcar, that this romance was destined not to succeed because of the cruel reality of horrid past events. Both formidable ladies Mayanèt and Elizi Dantò certainly guaranteed this failure. However, the idealistic young lovers were not interested in listening even when their much wiser elders tried to warn them, knowing that such folly would have dire consequences. *'Se le koulev mouri, ou konn longe li.'* ... Only when the serpent is dead can you measure it.

Within a few days after trying to cope with considerably weighty issues of shared histories and interconnecting identities, Alegra and Nelson were plagued with equal turbulence by the urgencies that initially had brought the two university students back to the *Isla* of their birth. When Alegra was selected to participate in her university's eagerly awaited and important research project to investigate the effects of recent indications of climate change occurring in the Caribbean, she, along with Nelson-- who decided that he didn't want to miss the chance to travel home -- had absolutely no inkling that their three-month stay would also take them both on an unanticipated secondary journey down a long, dark path of enormously shocking revelations. This 'unauthorized digression' in every sense would be transformational for the young couple.

The prestigious research team was headed up by some of the world's renowned climate scientists and uncompromising environmental activists of gigantic stature and respect. One team member, for instance, Ted De Christopher, had spent two years incarcerated in federal prison for his fervent activism-- some say 'stubborn activism.' Each of the other individuals serving on the team also had been arrested on numerous occasions for specific acts of civil disobedience regarding bringing public awareness to the pressing issues of climate change and global warming. The illustrious team also included Bobby McKibben, Naomi Stein, Van Jonesboro, Sally Halpern, and Maggie Oppenheimer. Also among the group of scientists were Kurtis Davies from the International Climate Investigations Center and Professor Robert Hansen, undoubtedly one of today's most prominent climatologist; his close friend and colleague Professor David Manning was also among the expert investigators.

Manning, unfortunately, had once been the selected target of obscene attacks -- the perpetrators were never revealed-- to discredit him and his brilliant research findings. For many years when Manning was a leading proponent of the real dangers of global warning, the overly zealous anti-science lieutenant governor of the particular state where he professor was teaching at the state university, launched a well-funded campaign to besmirch Manning's reputation. It was widely believed that the fossil fuel industry was directly responsible for this anti-climate change campaign. At any rate, the campaign was quite successful and the scholar was forced to abandon the state altogether.

As for Professor Hansen, as long ago as 1988, it was he who had informed the United States Congress about the world-wide consequences of global warming, saying audaciously, "the CEOs fossil fuel companies should all be tried for high crimes against humanity." He even referred to coal-fired power plants 'factories of death'. Remarkably fortunate for Alegra and Nelson, all these overwhelmingly unselfish and committed individuals were extremely effective in efforts to convince the young couple to re-focus their scholarly energies in the direction of the primary inventive for traveling back to the *Isla* in the first place... especially in Alegra's case.

Soon afterwards, call attention turned to what was a distressing alarm throughout the entire Island-- Alegra's and Nelson's *Isla.* The news centered upon the visible effects of the advancing *sequía.* The notices from the major media outlets were without exaggeration upon increase their coverage of the drought crisis with easily frightening detail.

"*Coastal water temperatures are rising and will continue rising by four degrees celsius by the end of the decade.*" The university research team now based on the Island was verifying this certainty occurring around the world; "*Arctic ice is melting fast,*" according to international climate science researchers. "*Arctic temperatures are therefore expected to be even lower than previously experienced."* As a consequence, temperatures around the globe are warming noticeably. *"Extreme weather conditions -- drought, fires, storms, rising ocean levels-- are now the new normal."*

Professor McKibben made a striking observation, "Whole economies are at risk because of the wide-ranging impact of climate change. We know that carbon dioxide in the atmosphere is extremely dangerous to fish and other life forms in the oceans and coral reefs." By now, Nelson and Alegra had regained completely their initial focus after being distracted in a major way by those other equally pivotal findings -- although of a delicately personal nature.

"The really sad and shameful fact about this global crisis," offered Alegra, "is that so far there's been no agreement whatsoever by world nations, especially the most powerful ones, to reduce greenhouse emissions. For starts, consider why this geographic region of our Caribbean was chosen for the investigations. We can see right here the devastating effects with the extreme heat and carbon emissions increasing at such dangerous levels."

"Look also at the flash flooding with the river system of the Isla; and there's no longer what used to be a true rainy season," added Nelson.

Another very alert student member of the team put forth another significant observation. "I certainly learned something I didn't realize before now: women comprise about 80% of the farmers in developing countries in Africa, Asia, and Latin America. And I'm learning that climate change is adversely affecting women in all areas of the world. This already vulnerable segment of the world's population-- women-- is the poorest and the hardest hit. So then, there is the likelihood of actual food insecurity ... food shortages. I don't see any sustainable future with this harsh reality staring us in the face."

Professor Hansen confirmed this proven fact, expressing his own indignation and fury.

"Then, of course, there's the fundamental question of the Kyoto Protocol, which was the very first agreement between nations to mandate country-by-country reductions in greenhouse-gas emissions. I was there in attendance; I wouldn't have missed it. That ground-breaking conference in Japan had emerged from the United Nations Framework Convention on Climate Change and was signed by nearly all the nations present at that important 1992 meeting called *'The Earth Summit.'* At the time, I certainly had my own reservations about this summit. For example, I felt that any kind of pledge to stabilize greenhouse gas concentrations at a level resulting in dangerous as interference with the climate system was filled with a great deal of doubt. After all, the inherent interests of corporate capitalism were and always will be more powerful than any sincere concern for eliminating human suffering. I honestly don't think the corporate elite care a damn about the legitimate rights and well-being of the world's populations as a whole."

Next, De Christopher interjected anxiously. "Perhaps not surprisingly, nearly all nations now have ratified the protocol... but with the notable exception of our colossal neighbor to the north, the United States. Developing countries, including China and India, weren't mandated to reduce emissions, given that they had contributed a relatively small share of the current century-plus buildup of carbon dioxide. And still, these carbon levels in our atmosphere, as we're now experiencing, are rising at a frightening rate with no sign of slowing down."

Alegra added, "How disgraceful that one of the worst offenders, the United States, continues blocking any meaningful action on climate change precisely because of selfish oil-rich, fossil fuel interests and profits. We've all noticed how nearly all of corporate media weather forecasts never even use the term *'climate change.'* And the notion of a present-day governor, twice-elected governor of Florida, in fact, has ordered his department heads, including the one that handles the state's environmental issues, to not even use the words *'global warming'* in any department reports. Can you begin to believe that? And in one of the states most directly impacted by rising coastal waters."

The invigorating exchange among the team members, students and professors alike, continued at length when Professor Manning made another point. "Progress was indeed slow and frustrating. How can any of us forget what recently happened at the Doha Conference on climate change. In the country of Qatar, an Arab country with the highest per capita emissions on the entire planet, what we have is an oil-producing country with a population of nearly two million and is the world's wealthiest country. Of course it's not difficult to be frustrated with the slow pace of progress; there is noticeable resistance by powerful countries and the seemingly low common denominator of international negotiations. But does it mean that we give up? Can the world's populations afford such a surrender? And especially the smaller, poorer countries like this beautiful paradise where we find ourselves at this very moment? Dammit, it's always the poorest nations, always the weakest ones that are made to suffer most and carry the heaviest burden.

And it was all quite true ... without exaggeration. Before the groundbreaking Doha Conference, there had been different groups divided by notions of 'fully developed and still-developing' countries. Now, there is but a single negotiation forum for all countries.

Noami Stein reminded the others, "This was no small achievement. Today, the average emission per capita in China, for instance, is already 7.2 tons and increasing. Europe's is 7.5 tons and decreasing. The world really cannot fight climate change without emerging economies being committed seriously in this struggle."

Alegra spoke up in frustration when she said emphatically, "I said to my mom and to everyone else recently that climate change is not a hoax. On the contrary, it's very real and it poses one of the biggest human rights struggles that we've known in the course of global social history. Our little *Isa* serves as immediate testimony."

All the professors and environmental activists, without exception and naturally without being prompted, expressed total satisfaction upon witnessing at close range how with each passing day the alert young scholars accompanying the adult experts were quickly becoming more acutely aware of the gravity of this global crisis. All the experienced adults said they were absolutely delighted in the way the students were now describing climate change as ... *"being equated with what correctly is nothing short of a crisis in climate justice."*

It was Jonesboro, the globetrotting activist, who then shared with the team a recent event where none-other-than England's Prince Charles was the surprise keynote speaker before a distinguished gathering of world health experts. Addressing the group at the Royal Society in London, the Prince began his talk with personal observations.

"In my view, a healthy planet and healthy people are two sides of the very same coin. We can only pray that one sick planetary patient might be placed on the road to recovery, in the tedious process of bringing gains for human well-being." He was speaking to strategically positioned individuals in the nation's health systems about the urgent need to place the issue of human health at the center of the climate change debate.

"I suggest to you, however, that our failure to write the prescription might sadly render us consider writing the inevitable death certificate instead."

There was every clear indication in Prince Charles's insistence that climate change is a realistic challenge of astonishing complexity, thus urging all health practitioners to be more courageous and fearless about highlighting its overwhelming effects on well-being.

Jonesboro shared further thoughts. "Clear enough," he said to the research team. "The fact of climate change is now accepted by every scientific body around the globe. There can hardly be any degree of accusation of a wide-spread conspiracy designed by so-called *'radical environmentalists'*– referring to us, of course-- intent upon somehow sabotaging and undermining capitalism" Jonesboro chuckled about such absurdity.

Alegra quickly added, "Nearly 97% of world experts have now reached a consensus on human-caused global warming. The real hoax is that fossil fuel-funded scientists and climate change deniers continue to receive disproportionate media coverage."

Nelson took his cue from his very confident sweetheart. "We've learned that climate scientists everywhere have linked the massive snowstorms, the flooding, and the unusually bitter spring weather recently experienced across Britain, and large sections of Europe and North America to the dramatic loss of Arctic sea ice. Both the extent and the volume of the sea ice forming and melting each year in the Arctic Ocean fell to an historic low last autumn".

"A terrible loss!" another student exclaimed. "This is a clear symptom of global warming, contributing to an increased warming of the Arctic, where ice loss adds heat to the oceans and atmosphere. This then shifts the position of the jet stream, thereby resulting in the extremes in weather that we are witnessing everywhere. What happens next is that the cold air plunges much further south. Here in the Caribbean, for example, that's why we're experiencing higher than usual ocean levels and dangerous flooding."

Maggie Oppenheimer offered an ominous warning, "The world can most certainly expect more extremes of weather -- record heat, more droughts, more life-threatening sea surges, more hurricanes. Period. These are the sorts of changes that are going to affect us in quite a short timescale ... starting right now."

Her colleague and friend Bobby McKibben was fiercely adamant when he reminded everyone that the global warming deniers have been handed a huge and powerful megaphone and that there doesn't remain an eternity to come to realistic grips with this irreversible crisis.

True enough, as everyone remembered how some of the biggest and richest fossil fuel companies in the world– during the mid-1990s— were devising ingenious schemes to hijack the science of human-caused global warming. Officials from major fossil fuel corporations, like the Coke Industries and the Haliburton Group, had aligned themselves with skillful operatives from influential U.S. conservative think tanks and public relations professionals to draft what they named their 'Global Climate Science Communications (GCSC) Project'.

It was Kurtis Davies who clarified, "Basically, this project audaciously declared its mission as being a plan to convince the majority of the American public that ... 'significant uncertainties and fallacies exist in climate science.'" Davies, a former Greenpeace chief researcher and founder of the Climate Investigations Center, not very long ago released to the world community a certifiable, scathing report ... thanks to the Freedom of Information Act ... a few major U.S. coal utility corporations had actually paid scientist Dr. William Soon, an acclaimed aerospace engineer based at the Harvard-Smithsonian Center for Astrophysics, more than $400,000 in recent years for 'science research.' Davies pointed out that Professor Soon had earned more than two million dollars from the coal utility, as well as from Exxon and the American Petroleum Institute in the last fourteen years. This particular scientist, Dr. Soon, is perhaps the media's most frequently-cited among the corps of climate scientist deniers claiming that... *"the sun is the key driver of climate change and thus fossil fuels play only a minor role."* Of course, most of the world's climate scientists– a reported 97%-- have repeatedly dismissed Dr. Soon's views.

DIECISIETE

Alegra shared with the team her report detailing what she and Nelson, still accompanying her everywhere the team's research tasks led, had observed on a recent trip to the western zone of the *Isla*.

"Exciting news!" she nearly screamed. "Our neighbors on the other side of the Artibonite River have proudly announced that the government, for the first time in its long history, intends planting more than fifty thousand trees yearly in a truly bold and ambitious reforestation campaign. The officials said that this massive tree-planting project will address one of the primary causes of the country's poverty and ecological vulnerability. The president is launching the drive with the goal of doubling forest cover by the year 2016 from the dangerous levels of just 2% -- one of the lowest rates in the entire world."

Nelson, along with the other student scientists, learned that Haiti, in its early colonial history, was once completely covered in lush, green forests; but the massive land clearance for colonial plantations was quickly followed by thoughtless tress felling for use as cooking fuel. Even today, most people—whether living in the rural zones or in urban areas — still use charcoal for their home cooking purposes. It is estimated that on a yearly basis from thirty to forty million trees are cut down on the Kreyòl-speaking side of the *Isla*. Shamefully, the national government has never intervened to stop this senseless destruction by simply providing the citizens everywhere with subsidized fuel for domestic needs. Solar, kerosene, and propane stoves seemingly would easily be sustainable alternatives to wood or charcoal cooking.

Today, any air passenger flying into the *Isla*, first crossing over the western third portion before entering the

Spanish-speaking side, is jolted by the shocking contrast. The high mountains and hills west of the Artibonite River offer a suddenly dreadful panorama of eeriness and emptiness because of seems like a permanent *sequía*; there are no trees or scrubs or woodland flowers, just total grayness, while the eastern side is visibly luxuriant with an excessive abundance of green forests and inviting carpets of emerald ground foliage. It's like two different worlds.

What Alegra said about what she and Nelson had witnessed on the other side of the border automatically reminded one of the other students of the heated controversy currently raging throughout the United States, involving cross-border issues and climate change.

"I can't believe that there is even a debate about the catastrophic consequences of climate change when it comes to extending the Canadian Tar Sands Pipeline System into the United States. This filthy, poisonous oil extraction, tar sands, is the largest and most destructive energy project in the word," the well-informed young scientist said with passion.

True enough; this toxic waste creates more greenhouse gas emissions than 140 nations combined. Everybody knows it is the dirtiest crude oil on the planet and the proposed 1,700-mile long Keystone XL Pipeline System is intended to transport this waste from Alberta, Canada all way to refineries situated in the Gulf Coast of Texas. This pipeline is designed to open up the vast store of carbon in the Alberta Tar sands — pumping up to 830,000 barrels a day to the Texas coast. And yet, there is much debate about the merits of the project, job creation versus reliance on foreign oil imports. Separating the oil from the rock is energy intensive, causing three to four times more carbon emissions per barrel than conventional oil. It would be 'game over' for the climate if tar sands were fully exploited, given that existing conventional oil and gas are certain to be burned in the process."

Professor Mann readily confirmed the point. "You're absolutely correct. The U.S. State Department, of course, is involved because the project crosses an international border. This, to me, is insanity at the highest level."

He made it clear that the Canadian government has been lobbying relentlessly as have the oil industry — reportedly with incentives of impressive sums of money — for the project. In addition, various Chambers of Commerce on both sides of the northern border have been directly engaged in the selling campaign. Environmental activists like Klein and Jones, also De Christopher, along with scores of other individuals bitterly opposed to the project, have staged regular protests outside the White House, urging the U.S. President to take bold, courageous action on climate change by rejecting outright the Pipeline. These undaunted voices are calling for the president to choose instead, a responsible path forward before climate disruption becomes unmanageably dangerous.

Jonesboro said, "In all honesty and in my heart, I believe this president will side with science and do what's in the best interest of the planet. This president will thus become the first president in history to take a definitive stand to stop human-caused climate change."

Klein made a significant point when she said, "I think the president achieved an enormously vital agreement with China to curb and reduce carbon pollution. The EPS's Clean Power Plan and the rejection of the Keystone XL would be a huge step in establishing a national policy to reduce our carbon emissions. Quite an ambitious proposal in reducing carbon emissions from our existing energy systems; also, the plan to reject tar sands infrastructure projects would make certain that we don't undermine those reductions in attempting to introduce new, dirtier fuel sources. There is no doubt that this president, by taking his determined action to veto the pipeline, would cement his legacy in a noble way."

McKibben asserted, "It is probable that the earth's ecosystem changes could recur ... as in this case with Keystone. We know that reef corals once suffered a major extinction while forests once grew up to the far northern edge of the Arctic Ocean ... a region that today is bare tundra. The extreme speed at which carbon dioxide is now rising — maybe 75 times faster than in pre-industrial times — has never appeared in geological records. Actually, we are already witnessing some effects of climate change when we see extreme heat waves and intense flooding now more frequent than ever before. Recent wet and cold summer weather in Europe, for instance, has been linked directly to radical changes in the high level jet stream, in turn, linked to the rapidly melting sea ice in the Arctic."

Nelson eagerly recalled, "And we can't forget about animal species that also will surely be hit by climate change. There's already been predictions that at least one-third of common land animals could see dramatic losses this century because of climate change, as habitats become unsuitable for many species. The total collapse of ecosystems have major economic impacts on air quality, agriculture, clean water access, and for us here on the *Isla* especially-- tourism."

Alegra was thus prompted to reflect back to her days at *La Morenita* and to those blissful early mornings with her adorable vervet monkeys and the soothing evenings that were forever filled with the cheerful sounds of evasive, rarely-seen, red-eyed tiny tree frogs, announcing their name ... *'coquí, coquí, coquí.'*

While still engaged in their intoxicating investigations on the *la Isla*, the team received the sobering -- but at the same time very distressing notice about global carbon dioxide in the atmosphere having passed the milestone level

"Climate warming greenhouse gas has now reached 400 parts per million (ppm) for the first time in human history! The last time so much greenhouse gas was in the air was time so much greenhouse

gas was in the air was several million years ago, when the Arctic was ice-free, savannah spread across the Sahara Desert and sea level was up to 40 meters higher than today's level."

According to all interpretations of the reporting, these levels are expected to return in time, with severely destructive consequences for the planet's civilizations unless emissions of carbon dioxide from the burning of coal, gas, and oil are drastically and rapidly curtailed. Despite increasingly dire warnings from distinguished climatologists around the world and a major global economic recession, harmful emissions everywhere have continued to soar unchecked.

With characteristic urgency, Professor McKibben pointed out a significant fact about passing this 400-point threshold. He said that it should serve as a vital wake-up call of the incredibly fast rate at which, and the extent to which we have increased the actual concentration of greenhouse gases in our atmosphere. At the state of industrialization in Western societies, the heaviest concentration of carbon dioxide was just 280.

"I can only hope that crossing this milestone will bring about serious awareness of the scientific reality of climate change and how human society must deal honestly and urgently with this challenge. This 400 ppm threshold is a sobering milestone and should serve as a wakeup call for all of us to support clean energy technology and meaningful emission reductions before it's too late for our children and grandchildren."

His colleague Manning agonized with equal insistence about the importance of having reached that milestone. One specific concern of Manning's was that climate change at this stage has begun to create a new kind of forced homelessness.

"Millions of people," he said, "are being displaced from their homes by the ruinous impact of rapidly changing climate. It is more than ever likely that hundreds of millions of people will be forced to abandon their homelands in the near future as a result of rising temperatures around the world."

Professor Manning elaborated on the fact that temperature were rising to frightening levels precisely because carbon dioxide levels were themselves rising. It is evidenced that this forced migration has already begun in certain areas around the globe where there are clearly disrupted weather patterns and spreading deserts. The unfortunate individuals living in such zones are referred to as *'climate refugees.'* For most people, the immediate image that comes to mind of 'climate refugees' is that of people living in those small, remote tropical islands --perhaps in the South Pacific or in those low-lying deltas such as in Bangladesh, where people have been forced from their homes by the unanticipated rise of sea-levels. But with climate change happening so fast in the far north and with temperatures warming much faster than the global average, the typical picture of the 'climate refuge' is about to become more diverse.

It was quite true; sea ice has been reported to be in fast retreat, and the permafrost is indeed melting. Alegra and Nelson, with other students attending their climate science lectures at the university, had seen filmed reports of remote village of Alaska that are already experiencing the unusual flooding and land erosion in that region. These students learned that, unlike all those folks in New Orleans who were forced by Hurricane Katrina to flee from their homes, nearly all the native Alaskans have occupied their ancestral homelands for centuries. Their forced exile is not provoked by a single cataclysmic event like Katrina showed. On the other hand, climate change in Alaska is proving to be a slow-moving disaster.

Nelson expressed a sound thought, "Not surprisingly, climate change remains politically a very touchy subject in Alaska."

In fact, all the other students noted that climate change is regarded as a hoax by many politicians... especially since the entire state of Alaska owes its enormous prosperity to the ongoing development of the massive Prudhoe Bay oil fields on the Arctic Coast. Perhaps the afternoon's culminating in the scholarly reporting came when one of Alegra's favorite professors made the observation about water shortages in the face of climate change. His opinion was that ... "most of the areas where water will be the scarcest are in poor countries around the globe ... in countries which naturally have very little resilience to cope."

More than 500 scientists have now warned that the majority of the Earth's nine billion people will live with severe pressure on potable water within the space of two generations as climate change, pollution and excessive utilization of resources take their worst toll. The world's water systems would soon reach a tipping point that could readily trigger highly irreversible change with potentially catastrophic consequences. These experts were solidly convinced that it was wrong to see fresh water as an endlessly renewable resource because, in many cases, people are pumping out water from underground sources at such a rate that it won't be restored within several lifetimes. These are really self-inflicted wounds.

The young researchers learned further that the majority of the population already live within about 50km of a so-called 'impaired water source.' Alegra was fortunate to have witnessed this fact personally during her transformative trip to Africa. A seriously impaired water source, as she saw, is one wherein the water system is running dry or is altogether polluted.

"If these trends continue," according to one professor, "millions more people will see the water — on which these people so desperately depend—simply running out or becoming so filthy that it no longer sustains life." Each professor delivered his or her presentation as if they were still in the university lecture hall.

"The run-off from agricultural fertilizers containing nitrogen has already created more than two hundred large so-called 'dead-zones' in seas and near river mouths, where fish can no longer survive. Inferior, cheap technology used for pumping water from underground and from rivers, and the few restrictions on the use of this technology has led to the excessive use of scarce resources or industrial purposes," one senior professor offered.

Alegra turned to Nelson, saying, "So then, as a direct result, much of that water is wasted because of inefficient techniques. In some cases, so much water would be pumped out from underground that salt water rushes in to fill the gap, and this will force farmers to have to move into other areas because the salinization makes their former water sources useless."

Nelson concluded. "There's no doubt that it will take genuinely concerned politicians and activists around the globe to decide to call for implementation of really tough new targets for improving water in sustainable development goals. These governments and NGO leaders, if they are honest in their concerns, must introduce water management systems that will address the interconnected crisis of pollution, waste, and climate change." Nobody present in the room was left without a realistic sense of urgency at the conclusion of this jolting delivery.

DIECIOCHO

The three months of intellectually challenging and intensive research, observation, and meticulous data collecting required diligent and unhampered focus on the parts of participating young student scientists. They all had listened with genuinely avid attention and interest; in turn, they were successful in bringing clarity to every fact and expert opinion heard during their university lectures. These young students were greatly impressed by what they gained overall from the brilliant assemblage of imminent scholars and committed activists heading the project. What a truly rare experience for these bright young students. Alegra, but also Nelson as an astute observer accompanying his sweetheart on the trip, were equally anxious about sharing every iota of these scientific revelations with their respective families once the multitude of tasks and responsibilities had ended.

There was no doubt that the young lovers were so thoroughly captivated by what they experienced while on the *Isa* together that they both all but forgot-- or at least were successful in shoving to one side for the remainder of their stay-- the other complicated and entangled family histories that had recently conquered the centerpiece of 'starting revelations.' Alegra and Nelson felt the stunningly visible and immediate urgencies of climate change more so than before returning to their native *Isla*.

"There is no citizen anywhere on the planet who can afford to be complacent about the very real challenges we face concerning climate change," Alegra was prepared to admit to her mother.

Nelson did not hesitate to add, "*Mi querida amor*, I suspect that with total disregard for such realistic challenges, there will still be skeptics and cynics everywhere who will continue believing that global warming is nothing but a cruel joke."

There was no attempt to hide his pessimism. The young couple was nevertheless thrilled about visiting their respective families again after spending so many mind-boggling, sometimes stressful and arduous weeks investigating the effects of global warming as evidence throughout the region. They decided to visit *La Morenita* first and go later to the town located considerable distance from where Nelson's family lived. Everybody was anxious to hear what their two stellar young climate scientists had learned on the highly publicized expedition. To the best of anyone's recollection, there had never been an event of such magnitude on their *Isla* ....except, though, if they excluded that memorable occasion many year ago when the when the young Canadian 'sugar doctor' first arrived from Toronto to conduct an investigation into the Island's sugarcane crop.

Azúcar was extremely proud, as also were Nelson's parents, but at the same time curious about what precisely what the two university students had learned from the experience of being in the company of those world famous 'weather experts'... as old *don* Anselmo referred to the research project. The exhilaration at *La Morenita* was as crisp and charged with the same momentum that had been generated three months earlier when everybody awaited Alegra's first trip back home since she had returned for her father's funeral. The welcoming reception on both occasions was joyous in every sense. As before, *'la famni sanble'*... the family assembled in hopes of hearing first-hand every detail that the young couple had to report about the intriguing climate investigations.

As anticipated, everybody demonstrated authenticate sensitivity in not mentioning a single word, nor made the slightest reference to the ill-fated romance between Alegra and the young student from the same *Isla* ... Nelson de la Rosa.

Azúcar and *don* Anselmo shared the thought that the sacred ancestral spirits, in their own time, would offer the proper guidance for navigating through this delicate course. Alegra began by highlighting for the *'famni'* a recently distributed World Bank Report that painted an incredibly bleak picture of the damaging effects of global warming on the most vulnerable regions of the planet. In graphic detail, according to the unnerving report, major Asian cities will find themselves completely underwater; millions of innocent people will be trapped in abject poverty; Africa will be plunged into severe drought and plagued by deadening food shortages; flooding will be of Biblical proportions. The undeniable central focus of the report reveal what will be the planet's reality well within our lifetime … due to global warming and climate change.

Nelson waited to add, "*Sí, es verdad lo que dice.* Yes, it's true what the report says; it shows exactly what a two-degree Celsius rise in global temperatures will do to our planet within the next twenty to thirty years." Many of the more frightening conclusions, most convincingly, speak for themselves. Events like that monstrous and deadly flooding of 2011, for instance--- directly affected twenty million people -- will certainly become common and the traditional monsoon season could bring an even worse crisis. Major cities like Manila, Mumbai, Calcutta, Ho Chi Minh City, and Bangkok could find themselves underwater or threatened by tremendous cyclones; by the 2030s, *sequías* and extreme heat will cause about forty percent of current maize-growing land to become useless. By the 2050s, depending on where an observer is located on the continent, the part of the population that already is undernourished will increase by about twenty-five to ninety percent.

"And look at what happened a few weeks ago in northern India, a region surrounded by the majestic Himalayas... terrifying floods that killed at least 5,000 people while many thousands more are still unaccounted for," continued Alegra.

"It's happening all over the world. The more that we strip the natural environment, the smaller and more defenseless the buffer zones become. Where the forests of certain regions are being cut down senselessly, the less protection there is from extra heavy rains.

Alegra offered yet another poignant example of negative consequences of global warming as she called everybody's attention to what was occurring in Malaysia at the moment. A state of emergency has been declared now that thick haze from fires on the nearby island of Sumatra caused harmful smog to drift over Singapore and Malaysia; the worst pollution levels ever are a direct result.

After offering a wider, more global perspective of hard evidences of climate change, Alegra and Nelson paused deliberately so that these specific instances might better resonate with the assembled listeners ... eager as they were to hear more of this reporting. The two anxious reporters wanted to shift the focus onto the more immediate concern– the increasing threat of climate change to their own Caribbean region. Nelson began with a truly provocative question.

"Did you know that lately thousands of people on the tiny island of Grenada see themselves literally having to move away from the coastal zones? Fishermen, for example, who have lived for generations all along that island's coasts are now seeing a sudden and dangerous rise in sea levels. This is not some kind of textbook theory; rather, it's actually happening there, as those fishermen told us directly."

"*Coño! El maldito mar se va a llevar todo.* [Dammit! The cursed sea is going to carry away everything!]," muttered *don* Anselmo in a low, hardly audible voice. He directed his angry remark to no one in particular, but at the same time, to everybody assembled. This was also what those fishermen on Grenada had said, realizing that they all were being 'evicted' from their ancestral space ... being forced to more further inland to higher, safer ground. Azúcar's brilliant young climate scientist was thoughtful to remind everybody how the almost total destruction of Grenada during the deadly assault of Hurricane Ivan back in 2004 showed tragically the stark reality of the susceptibility of all the Caribbean Islands, large and small alike.

Everybody could easily see for themselves that storms on Alegra's and Nelson's *Isla* were becoming more violent and occurring more often; beach erosion was happening everywhere and faster than ever before. Highly respected climate experts like the ones the two young scholars accompanied on the research team all agreed that these conditions, along with steadily rising sea levels, could radically transform the *Isla's* coasts over the coming decades.

In turn, these changes are certain to generate truly horrific socio-economic hardships for everybody. The Caribbean, with nearly total dependence on tourism, is considered one of the most endangered regions in the world today.

Nelson was equally confident and poised when it became his turn to share what he had also learned. He moved toward the large globe of the Earth, nestled comfortably on its sturdy wooden easel, displayed prominently in front of the large panoramic window of the handsome family room. He wanted to talk about another island in order to illustrate the realistic impact of climate change; he pointed to a site on the globe -- the Maldives. It can rightfully be said that these remote islands may be considered ground zero for climate change impacts. It is a place that many people may possibly have heard of, but few can easily locate on a map. These islands are as flat as pancakes... comprising twelve hundred islands and atolls -- the ring-like coral islands and reefs that nearly or entirely enclose a lagoon; but only two hundred of these are inhabited today. The highest one is no more than about five feet above sea level, making the Maldives the lowest-lying country on the globe. And so, the Maldives are among the most threatened by potential sea level rise. Lately as these rising sea levels and warmer ocean surface temperatures have grabbed more and more headlines, so has this tiny island nation.

In a truly moving speech before the United Nations General Assembly, President Mohamed Nasheen of the Maldives warned sternly, "What happens in the Maldives today, happens to you tomorrow." Once, in order to illustrate in a uniquely dramatic fashion to the world community that his tiny nation was already beginning to sink, President Nasheen actually held a session of parliament underwater ... with all his assembled MPs dressed in full undersea gear! Everybody thought correctly that the president had made his point.

"During the course of our observations particularly along the southwestern coast of our own *Isla*, we recorded disturbing numbers of dead dolphins and rotting fish," Alegra alerted everyone, bringing attention to the urgency on a local basis. She emphasized how rapidly warming ocean temperatures throughout the Caribbean could lead to a more frequent sight on the region's otherwise pristine beaches such as she described.

"If the prediction is that drastically changing climate patterns are going to leave warmer waters and algae blooms remaining for months at a time, then this occurrence is definitely going to affect the natural aquatic habitat of these sea creatures," she noted. Together, she and Nelson hoped to convince their listeners that ... *"humans are the only species that takes, consumes, and destroys without creating anything that helps the planet grow."*

This profound thought has always been the pivotal theme for several participating members of the visiting research team. One professor regularly made the disturbing observation that "We are the most intelligent species and the one most likely to outlive any other; we are also the only species that, in the future, may be able to combat the increase in global warming to the benefit of the entire planet.

"*Carajo!* So then, we are like a growing cancer," *don* Anselmo erupted angrily in his customary manner.

"*Es verdad*, it's true," replied Alegra as if to confirm the old man's observation while seeming to summarize all that she and Nelson had outlines.

"For that reason, climatologists are forecasting dangerously rising global temperatures, leading inevitably to real catastrophe across large areas of the Earth. Just look at this terrible *sequía* that we're facing right here. Everybody is admitting the obvious truth; the *Isla* has never known these kinds of extreme weather conditions before ... more frequent and fiercer storms, uncontrollable flooding, unbearable heat waves, and unbelievable rises in ocean levels."

Nelson was even more poignant. "In our south-west, from the dry Bahoruco and Pedernales zones and all the way into Haiti's eastern *Massif de la Selle*, considering the likelihood of a drier future with increasing demand for water, groundwater loss and higher temperatures will raise the impacts of future droughts. Researchers already have predicted that that particular region of our *Isla* will face decade-long *sequías* far worse than any experiences over the last 1,000 years because because of climate change. It will become practically impossible to continue with current life-as-normal conditions in that part of the *Isla*.

Don Anselmo offered another conclusive personal assessment. "I'm convinced that for the first time in the history of the human species we have developed the capacity to destroy ourselves.

Alegra followed up on the old man's notion of the inevitability of self-destruction. "There is a war going on all over the world --- a major war over direct environmental destruction."

Nelson agreed solidly with his sweetheart. "In societies where indigenous populations have a realistic influence, many people are taking a strong stand regarding global warming. Without any question in my mind, Bolivia is demonstrating the strongest resistance. Under the historic leadership of President Evo Morales-- the first indigenous national president in the Americas in over four hundred years-- there are actual constitutional mandates that protect the 'Right of Nature.'"

Alegra hastened in mentioning, "Then there is the very bold example of Ecuador. This is another majority indigenous country and the only oil exporter where the national government under leftist President Rafael Correa is seeking aid to keep that oil in the ground, instead of producing and exporting it; and the ground is where it belongs."

"There is the case of the late Venezuelan President Hugo Chávez -- who died recently and was the object of a consistently sinister campaign of vilification, ridicule and insult, even outright hatred by the United States media and several other Western governments. Venezuela, of course, is a major oil producer, with almost their entire gross domestic product centering on oil. A few years before his death, Chávez gave a monumentally significant speech before the U.N. General Assembly-- a speech that was not covered by most of the Western press. He warned at the time of the dangers of overuse of fossil fuels and urged all the producers and consumer countries to come together to try finding solutions to reduce fossil fuel use."

"It's more than ironic," Harold pondered aloud. "At one extreme we have indigenous societies trying to stem the maddening race toward total destruction. At the other end, the richest, most powerful societies in all of world history, like the United States and Canada, are racing at full-speed to destroy the environment as fast as possible. They are undoubtedly driven solely by mind-boggling profits and naked greed. Unlike both Ecuador and Bolivia, these powerful countries want to extract every possible drop of hydrocarbons from the ground as fast as modern technology will allow."

"Peyi-ap fini nan lanmé [The country is going to end up in the sea.]", was Marcelo's unexpected and truly unusual response. This traditional Kreyòl saying was normally reserved for *'el viejo sabio del batey* ... to pulling it from his amply stocked treasure chest of highly valued verbal gems. The old man

always used to apply this particular expression -- one of his most favorite -- to situations whereupon he felt overwhelmed by what he saw as the absurdity of human behavior. But Marcelo now found himself experiencing that same sense of futility and frustration, while Alegra refused to allow herself to be defeated. With firm resolve, she replied to Marcelo's claim. "Climate change is definitely happening here and now, right on our own *Isla,* but we can confront the carbon emissions rise; it's easy to feel powerless as catastrophe looms overhead."

Nelson also presented his determined refusal to be conquered by the onslaught of dire predictions. It was clear that he had learned volumes of new information upon accompanying Alegra and the university's research team back to the place of his birth. "Alegra is right," he commented to everybody, still listening intensively.

"Climatologists tell us that things will get much worse. This present *sequía* in which we find ourselves is just the beginning of things to come. But there are certain clear measures that we can take to meet this change. We can start by educating the folks around us ... by allowing the hard reality to sink in ... by convincing folks to accept the reality. We must remain alert to the ways that the climate crisis may present itself in our lives, thereby being better prepared and more resilient. After all, resilience has traditionally been at the very core of our existence and endurance on this *Isla.*" Nelson was almost defiant in delivering his concerns at this point.

Alegra forcibly harnessed herself against bursting forward with kisses for him. She wanted to affirm Nelson's urgency when she added, "Populations around the globe, and led by students like ourselves, along with our professors and supportive activists must decide to take a stand. We must be genuinely committed to block extraction, transportation, burning of fossil fuels wherever it's occurring. In the United States, for example, concerned citizens are doing everything possible to stop the Keystone XL Pipeline and block fracking-- which falsely is claimed to be a *'climate-friendly alternative'* to coal and oil. However, in reality it isn't not. It's already a proven fact that a leakage of methane during the extraction process and then the actual shipment makes it as destructive to the climate as other fossil fuels-- threatening ground water supplies as well. Around the world, we've got to find sustainable ways to replace the consumer-oriented, energy-intensive life styles that are unaffordable both for our families and for future generations. Ultimately, it becomes a matter of the very survival of our planet." Everyone's eyes were downcast at this point... or so it seemed. There was little, if any question, that the atmosphere in the room was one of gloom; everybody felt it.

EPÍLOGO

There was an uncommon, rather eerie silence now dominating the space at *La Morenita* where once again *'la famni'* had assembled. However, the gathering this time preceded Alegra's departure. The climate science research project focusing on the uniqueness of the Caribbean region had come to its inevitable termination, and all the participants were preparing to return to their respective home universities, individual research centers, and private foundation headquarters. The young science students, each thoroughly equipped with invaluable new findings in addition to storing unforgettable, transformative experiences, were all very eager to begin their upcoming semester. Neither Alegra nor Nelson was necessarily excited to leave *la isla* since so many other unanswered questions begging for clearer explanations remained for the two young lovers. They both knew that a multiplicity of disturbing personal issues were yet to be sorted out; they both had hoped to have more substantial, satisfactory resolution before leaving now that the rigors of the extensive investigation had served only to spark further inquisitiveness.

At any rate, Alegra and Nelson were as anxious to share the results of the investigation as when the two first arrived, excited to reveal the precise nature of the project itself. Moreover, the two young scholars very proudly wanted to offer their personal perspectives about global warming affecting not only their native *Isla*, but also those real evidences of climate changes within the wider global context. The silence that greeted the young scientists' reporting was powerful to the extent that everybody was completely vanquished by the impact.

An unbiased observer might even admit that a distinct sense of despondency hovered precariously over the magnificent family room at *La Morenita* Estate. There was no mistaking about what everybody felt. What was also unmistakable was the silence that could be validated by the noticeable absence of the customary chatter and flutter of the array of tropical birds and small animals that were regularly present there. This was quite true during early morning, then again at mid-afternoon once the blazing sun, at its zenith, had decided to end its unintentional torment upon the humans below. Even the familiar frisky little vervet monkeys that routinely scampered with such maddening raucousness through the mango trees adorning the veranda made Alegra ask, "Where are my little friends?" First *don* Anselmo, then Azúcar became fully aware of the uncanny silence produced by the absent family of vervets that seemed to have gone into exile.

"*Ay, mi querida hija*. Oh, my dear child. Things just don't seem right to me. I know you and I can't be the only ones wondering, '*Qué carajo está pasando aquí?*' [What in Hell is going on here?]" However pesky these little creatures were, their constant, yet harmless annoyance paled considerably against the backdrop of this deafening silence precisely because of their absence.

Don Anselmo noted with nervous puzzlement, "*Por todos los santos*, in all my long years on this '*maldita Isla*', I can't remember when it was ever this damned quiet around here."

"*Es verdad*. It's true," Azúcar agreed. "Never before in my own memory have I not heard the familiar chirping of our feathered neighbors. I always saw *La Morenita* as a kind of private aviary since when '*mi querido*' Lucien built this spectacular home for us as a wedding gift so many years ago. I can't imagine what my *abuelita* Fela would have to say about all this."

Now, everybody's attention was drawn to the unavoidable quietness engulfing *La Morenita*, inside as well as outdoors. "There's no question, this is really strange," someone said without hesitating. But despite everything else mentioned, there was both consensus and insistence that Alegra continue with the eagerly awaited report. Not surprisingly, it was Nelson alone who was aware that during the course of Alegra's delivery, she clearly omitted a vital section of the otherwise official summary team report. For whatever her personal motives, Alegra failed to incorporate into her erudite summary, undeniably the most relevant portion of the investigation-- relevant as it impacts very decidedly the entire populations of their Caribbean Islands. Nelson felt that Alegra's reasoning for the omission had much more to do with her own skepticism rather than with anything possibly suggesting sheer negligence.

Her serious reservations about one specific item in the team's official final report resulted from her not wishing to provoke inadvertently any level of fear in her mother, whose current physical conditional and emotional state were becoming noticeably more delicate. Alegra, for this reason alone, secretly wanted to remain longer on the *Isla* in order to be at her mother's side. At the same time, Alegra had no intention of allowing any undue angst to overwhelm the other members of her beloved *familia*. Nelson naturally thought about his own family and also about exactly how they too would react to this particular omitted section of the report. He therefore softened his stance as he reflected thoughtfully. It was something that both Professors Manning and Hansen had presented rather pedantically during the final session of the research team before everyone departed. The information was frightening.

"Within only a few minutes' warning, a fifteen-foot-high wall of raging water... or to put it another way, a true *tsunami*, will shatter the normal tranquility of these lovely islands," the professors each took turns delineating.

The delivery by each of the respected climate exports was detached scientifically, without embellishment or personal sentiment; it was straightforward. Manning became more forceful. "We're referring mainly to the island of Guadeloupe to begin with. A new study reveals that the *tsunami* is expected to be generated when a tremendous landslide on the island of Dominica -- the largest and most mountainous of the Anglophone Windward group-- only thirty miles long and sixteen miles wide and whose highest peak is often covered entirely in mist--- plunges up to a million tons of solid rock into the sea. It isn't a case of *'if'* the landslide and *tsunami* will happen, but *'when.'* Most likely it will be triggered by a major undersea earthquake."

Hansen followed his colleague without a pause in the gripping delivery. "It could happen in a hundred years, next week, or next month; we can't say for certain, but it will definitely happen."

Without exaggeration, both Alegra and Nelson were overcome by a level of naked terror well beyond anything they had known previously in their young lives. The pronouncement by the two professors produced unbridled fear among the listeners. What happened was this: when the expert investigators had earlier surveyed the *Isla,* using the most highly sophisticated technology that produced amazing satellite images, the professors gained a bird's-eye view of rock outcrops normally obscured by dense vegetation. Both experts noticed that the north coast of all the islands under observation was unusually straight, clearly indicating very active earthquake faults. Furthermore, close investigations on the ground revealed large tension cracks along the flank of a prominent volcano, Pico Duarte, the highest geographical point located on *don* Anselmo's and Azúcar's island paradise, thus convincing the observers of the certain landslide threat.

"No matter precisely when the landslide strikes, "the professors concluded," all the islands in the region would be at the mercy of any potential *tsunami*."

How could Alegra or Nelson possibly manage to revel any of this startling information to their loved ones? Despite their solid scientific formation and thorough confidence with all that they had learned during their academic study of climate science... and also given Alegra's personal and up-close experiences at some rather spectacular, eye-opening, geographic sites around the world, there was nevertheless genuine terror in what she and Nelson had just heard. They were both well aware that many scientists consider the *tsunami*... "the deadliest and most merciless of Nature's terrifying disasters... that few sights would be more horrific than giant sea walls moving toward shore at about six hundred miles per hour, in just three to five minutes, and traveling faster than a modern jet plane. The *tsunami* possesses a murderous fury, arriving completely without warning, quickly gathering speed as it travels... cresting at times to waves well over one hundred feet high. These waves can unleash unimaginable amounts of energy, swallowing up absolutely everything in its relentless path. The incredible pressure of water reaches the surface and spreads out unpredictably in all directions. The countless populations are literally paralyzed by the mere sight of this monstrous gush of water would not stand any possible change of survival."

Returning to the spiritual and psychological drought underway on the parts of both Alegra and Nelson, this particular crisis was worsening on several levels. The young lovers were met with increasing disappointment and desperations in their efforts to uncover certain long-held secrets, half-truths, and more specific answers to many still elusive questions. They were unable to unravel any clearer explanations regarding their confusing, complicated and interwoven past histories on their *Isla*. This shared history-- as is not uncommon in traditional island societies-- involved a seemingly endless list of principal, but also subordinate players in the convoluted family drama.

Alegra, for instance, had wanted so much to learn more about her mother's formative years spend in the *batey* and about what it really was like working at such an innocent young age in the sugarcane fields. She couldn't imagine her mother working like that. She was equally intrigued about the deeply revered, almost saintly *doña* Fela, her great-grandmother. Even the ignominious *batey* settlement itself seemed more like a wonderful invention of a fictional writer's imagination than the nightmarish reality that it truly was, according to the painful accounts of the survivors of that place and time.

There were names from that remote past that she had heard mentioned... persons she wished she had known, but wanted to be able to see their faces: Lolita and her self-described 'beautiful Haitian husband' Estimé; one-eyed Clementina, a trusted friend and neighbor to *doña* Fela and young Azúcar; the notoriously bad [but in a good sense], big-bosomed Serafina; Cirilo and his long-necked wife Teresa; Yvette Origèn-Desgraves and Mamá Lola; and most certainly, there was that single name that stood above the rest and regarded as the personification of evil itself, Diego Montalvo, the *'capataz'* [overseer] at *Esperanza Dulce* sugarcane plantation. The key protagonist in this human drama, undeniably, was the century-old *Esperanza Dulce*, once the most productive and most profitable plantation in the entire *Isla*. Just a single question about each of these names easily provoked a follow-up question of equal relevance and importance.

For Nelson's part, he too was left with any number of incomprehensible explanations and inconclusive answers to the mystery of their respective origins and connections. He too was fascinated by the obscure tales of characters such as Yvette Origèn-Desgrave, as well as by the many tales referred to as 'sacred ancestral spirits' such as Ogun, Danbala, Grann Oyá, Bawon Samdi, and perhaps most mystifying of all... by what were known as the 'two powerful ladies' Mayanèt and Ezili Dantò; also such places called Kalfou and Ginen seemed mythical. So much remained a dizzying labyrinth for Nelson. How desperately he now wanted now to resume the slow task of peeling away the cumbersome layers of the enigmatic history of events that implicated the families of both Alegra and Nelson.

These were events that occurred years before their respective births and far beyond the scope of what they had already discovered, as agonizing as that discovery was. But regrettably, the allotted time for the university project to be engaged in the region had expired, and so all the team members were focusing on resuming their lives upon leaving the Island.

Once removed by a few thousands of miles from the epicenter of the terror, the two young lovers, along with everyone else around the world, awoke one morning to incredibly shocking news. The traumatizing headlines announced the event without overstatement.

> *"CARIBBEAN ISLANDS HIT BY*
> *MONSTROUS TSUNAMI!"*
> *"NO REPORTS OF SURVIVORS"*
> *"THE ISLANDS SEEM TO HAVE*
> *DISAPPEARED FROM THE MAP!"*

The notice seemed beyond the surreal. The recorded, decisive date for the formation of the modern Caribbean was 1492, when the Italian navigator Cristóbal Colón [known in English as Christopher Columbus, of course], ambitiously underwritten by the powerful Spanish Monarchs Fernando and Isabela, successfully crossed the Atlantic Ocean and made that historic landfall in the Antilles. As a result of very lengthy archaeological investigations, we know now that there were countless indigenous cultures already living for centuries in the region; even given regular genocide campaigns to rid the Islands of the presence of these original groups, significant cultural traces remained until the time of the European invasion. At the moment of his initial arrival, Columbus is reported to have summarized his personal impression of the wondrous sight that greeted his crews by uttering a one-word description: *"Asombroso!"* [Astonishing!] Of course, *'El Gran Almirante'* ['The Great Admiral'] had no clue whatsoever of the fact that the Caribbean Sea was geologically separate from the North and South American continents... and that together with the isthmus of the land mass of Central America, it formed a tectonic plate, moving West at about four-to-five centimeters a year.

At the same time, the North American and South American plates, lying directly under the continents, and the Eastern half of the Atlantic Ocean, moving westward. We also now know that most of the Caribbean Islands were close to the boundaries of the Caribbean plate.

These plate boundaries are quite active; this is why most parts of the Caribbean have experienced frequent earthquakes, and why there were always a number of active volcanoes in the region. All the Windward Islands and most of the Leeward Islands, have had clear signs of geologically recent volcanic activity. This, and so much more, was at the very core of Alegra's and Nelson's university studies.

Alegra screamed loudly and seemingly uncontrollably, while Nelson merely stood totally bewildered and without saying anything at all; he was in a daze. There were no words that could conceivably express the immediate horror they both felt upon reading the jolting news about their native *Isla*. The tears pouring from the young science students continued without end. As Alegra and Nelson hugged each other tightly, looking directly into the now drenched eyes of the other, they seemed to want to ask, "How did you and I manage to escape this unbelievable nightmare?" Neither one, quite naturally, had any rational explanations. But the revered, wise elders, *'los viejos sabios'* from that bygone era of the *batey*, without hesitation, would have known to respond.

"Por el amor de todos los santos." It has been the unquestioned will of the sacred ancestral spirits to preserve and to protect this special young couple, both of them born of this *Isla*, so that they alone would be the ones responsible for recording accurately really happened here." *Don* Anselmo always used

to warn everybody, *"Peyi-ap fini nan lanmè."* So then, there was no surprise, and certainly it was certainly no mere coincidence that these two precious young Island jewels should be blessed so generously by the ancient sacred spirits in being permitted to depart safely from their *Isla* in this ordained and timely manner. They had been purposely spared *Bondye's* clearly apocalyptic act of vengeance.

Somewhere in the far reaches of the Caribbean Diaspora, far removed from the final devastation, three humble, devout Catholic nuns were huddled together, and with individual resoluteness, were reading selected passages from their Holy book about ...*'God's turning deserts into pools of water and the parched and into flowing springs.'* The nuns knew all too well that the hand of their God was responsible for the calamity in their beloved Caribbean.

And still elsewhere in another distant part of that same cultural diaspora there was yet another huddled group of devout souls; their origins were that same shattered region that was no more. These nervous individuals, still experiencing shock and total disbelief, had all assembled to petition their *Isla's* sacred ancestral spirits for forgiveness.

With heavy tears streaming down the face of each devout supplicant, they chanted between controlled bursts of mournful sobs the traditional words that painfully reminded everyone that ... *'going home is not, nor ever again will be a reality; nor would be the notion of locating and defining family.'*

"La fanmi sanble, sanble nan. Se kreyòl nou ye. Pa genyen Ginen ankò."

[The family is assembled, gathered in. We are Creoles who no long have Africa.]

Taking place in faraway Stockholm, Sweden, at the same time, was a very important gathering. The world's most eminent climatologists in attendance were unveiling their strongest warning to date about the disastrous consequences of human-caused climate change if drastic efforts worldwide are not adopted to slash greenhouse gas emissions. If the public and policy makers need a single adjective to describe the finding of the Intergovernmental Panel on Climate Change's new assessment report... the word is *'unequivocal'*. The prestigious Stockholm assembly expressed with more certainty than ever before-- with a 95 to 100 percent certainty that... *"humans are responsible for global warming. Our assessment of the science finds that the atmosphere and ocean have warmed to extreme levels, the amount of snow and ice has diminished, the global mean sea level has risen and the concentration of greenhouse gases have increased."*

The evidence for this assessment has grown, thanks to more and better research and observations, a much improved understanding of the climate system response and greatly improved climate models. "Continued emissions of greenhouse gases," according to the report, "will cause increased warming and radical changes in all components of the climate system. Limiting climate change will require substantial and sustained reductions of dangerous greenhouse emissions. The world's scientists have spoken

"Climate change poses a severe and immediate threat to our future and that of the planet itself." But the ancient spirits on so many occasions in the past also tried to warn us.

¡Y así que se acabó todo! ... And this is how everything came to an end!

****

Readers' Guide to Caribbean Cultural and Linguistic Terms

SPANISH TERMS

abuela (abuelita) grandmother (dearest grandmother)

azúcar sugar

azúcar morena little brown suga

barrio neighborhood

batey during pre-Columbian Amerindian (*Taíno*) origin, the word referred to an open-air commons area within the indigenous settlement used interchangeably as a ceremonial ball court and open market; later it became the area of living quarters for sugarcane workers; today, the *batey* is synonymous with the squalid, substandard housing for recruited agricultural workers.

Bosque de Flores Flower Forest

bracero a day-laborer; from the Spanish word meaning 'arm' (*brazo*), referring to brute force, physical labor usually associated with agricultural workers

caña de azúcar sugarcane

capataz during the era of plantation slavery, this individual was the oversee; today, simple 'the boss' or 'crew leader'

carajo/coño goddammit!

cojones testicles; *¡Qué cojones tienes!* 'What nerve you have!'

'El Corte' 'The Cutting' was the State-sponsored genocide campaign of Dictator Rafael Trujillo (Dominican Republic) against Haitians and Dominican-Haitians living in Dominican territory, especially the border zones (1937); called **'Koup Kouto'** ("Blows of the Knives') in Haitian Kreyòl.

conuco the traditional small vegetable garden for household consumption, usually planted at the side of the family house.

dominico-haitiano (Dominican-Haitian), a Dominican of Haitian parentage/descent born in Dominican territory, but regularly denied Dominican citizen; in 2005 the Dominican Supreme Court upheld the constitutionality of a new immigration law reinforcing the 'statelessness' and exclusion of thousands of Haitians and Dominico-Haitians living in the DR.

La hierba mala nunca muere 'Weeds never die.'

maldita cursed, damned

Mientras que haya vida, siempre habrá esperanza. 'As long as there is life, there will always be hope.

mi querido(a) my darling

paro general a general strike; a work stoppage

por el amor de mi alma for the love of my soul

por mi santísima madre for the sake of my most saintly mother

por todos los santos for the sake of all the saints

¡Qué bendición de dios! What a blessing from God!

el sabio viejo del barrio the neighborhood's wise elder/ the wise old man from the neighborhood

La Tierra de Nadie 'No Man's Land'; refers to the unclaimed/ unmarked land area between Haiti and the Dominican Republic

trigueño a complexion coloring resembling dark wheat

la zona franca the free trade zone where hundreds of multinational export assembly plants are located, offering low-wage employment wage

la zona fronteriza the border zone

¿Y es fácil? 'And you think it's easy?' —meaning the exact opposite: 'It's really difficult.'

yola makeshift raft (some say 'boat') used in traveling without official documentation across the shark-infested Mona Strait from the Dominican Republic to Puerto Rico

HAITIAN KREYÒL [CREOLE] TERMS AND TRADITIONAL HAITIAN SAYINGS

Anonse, o zanj nan dlo Oh Angels, underneath the water

an bad dlo refers to the sacred place where the ancestral spirits live; 'under the sea' or 'on the other side'

Bay kou bliye, pot mak sonje. 'Those who give out the blows forget while those who bear the scars remember well.'

coumbite /konbit collective solidarity; traditional Haitian way of neighbors in rural areas working together to accomplish a common objective.

Creole/Kreyòl Simply stated, Creole languages are essentially a 'contact language' or 'pidgin' language that developed for expediency in matters of trade or other 'contact' situations wherein different groups of speakers do not share any common languages, thus having to create a new means of communication. Creoles [the language, not the people] are pidgins that have expanded both their linguistic structures and their communicative functions, resulting in the native (principal) language of an entire speech community. Haitian Kreyòl is a member of the group of French-based creoles because an important part of its lexicon come directly from the French. Kreyòl should not be considered a dialect.

dechoukaj traditional act of uprooting trees, destroying in decisive manner to make way for new planting; in modern times, street reprisals employed against Duvalier's *tonton macoute* during and after the revolution that toppled the presidency of Jean-Claude Duvalier; the so-called 'necklace' was a rubber tire placed around the victim's neck and then set afire.

Depi gen lavi, gen espwa. 'As long as there is life, there is hope.'

Dlo kler va kouole devan ou. 'Clear water will flow in front of you ... and then everything will be made clear to you.'

kleren raw sugarcane liquor, made from the sap of the sugarcane

Kochon-yo kontan; men moun-yo pa kontan. 'The pigs are happy, but the people are not.'

Kon sa la yè. 'That's just the way it is.'

Jou va, jou vien; m'pa di passé ça. 'The days may come and go, but just wait; my day is coming soon. [The speaker expects ultimately to have her/his revenge.]

La famni samble. The family is gathered together … to hear something of much importance for the entire community.

lwa [lwas] 'spirits'; these are the divine entities who govern the cosmos according to sacred Vodou traditions. [n Spanish, '*loas*']

Malè pa gin klaksonn. 'Disasters always arrive unannounced.'

Mwin ginyin la pè; sé oun lavi' ki rèd. 'Life is difficult and I share so much of your pain.'

prêt savann itinerate country priest; official of the Vodou temple [ounfò] in rural areas; he recites Catholic prayers before beginning the traditional Vodou ceremonies as well as at community funerals and baptisms.

Pa bliye sa ma di w. 'Don't forget what I'm telling you.'

Paròl gin pié-zel. 'Words have feet and wings. [Be careful about you say.]

Tout komplis nan mizè nou. 'All of us are complicit in our misery.'

Se on ki pou mété lod lan sa. 'We are the ones who will straighten things out.'

Sonia Pierre [1974-2012] Dominican-Haitian social-political activist who championed Human rights for Dominico-Haitians; her uncompromising efforts were constantly and fiercely repudiated by Dominican officials; she was vilified by the Dominican press and many people who regarded her as a 'traitor' and 'enemy of the State.' Pierre's work earned her the 2006 Robert F. Kennedy Human Rights Award and the 2012 International Women of Courage Award.

Vodou but <u>never</u> the offensive 'Voodoo', which is the vilified, Hollywood-created corruption of the word. Vodou literally means 'spirit.' It is a highly complex amalgam of spiritual beliefs and rituals, giving meaning to life; African captives largely from the Congo and Dahomean [currently named Benin] regions of Western Africa brought traditional beliefs to Hispaniola [Haiti and Dominican Republic] during the island's colonial period [1492-1804]. *Vodouissants* [congregants of Vodou say they do not <u>practice</u> their religion, but rather, <u>live it daily</u>; it is regarded as a way of life.

VODOU DIVINITIES AND RELATED TERMS REFERENCED IN *'SEQUÍA'*

Baka an evil spirit which roams at night, taking the form of an animal

Bawon [Baron] Samdi chief spirit of the cemetery

Bondye the all-powerful deity at the head of all the Vodou pantheons; ruler of the universe [from the standard French *'Bon Dieu'* = Good/Gracious God]

Danbala serpent deity associated with water, the rainbow wisdom

Ezili Dantò [Erzulie], mother-warrior spirit usually imaged as dark-skinned, known for her fierce protectiveness; often regarded as the beautiful water goddess of love

Gede family of trickster spirits associated with ancestral dead, with sexuality, and with children

Ginen 'the abyss'... ancestral West Africa, original home of the sacred spirits, said to be underwater, below the earth; Guinea

kalfou/ kafou intersection or crossroads

Legba revered guardian of gates and doorways/liaison for souls on their journey to the sacred world of the spirits ... *'an bad dlo'*

Marasa sacred twins; **Marasa Bwa**, 'Twins of the Forest'; reference to ancient, secret ritual that sacrifices twin babies in order to protect the entire community from assault, harm, shame ... if the twins were born of a 'bad seed' [*e.g.*, their birth resulted from the mother's having been raped]

Mayanèt very powerful spirit, sometimes angry and vengeful, but also often sweet, protective and merciful, often conspiring with Ezili Dantò

****

About the Author

ALAN CAMBEIRA, born in Samaná, República Dominicana, holds an M.A. and a Ph.D. in Latin American/ Caribbean Studies, and lectures regularly on cultural and socio-political issues of the region. His literary works, published in English, Spanish, and French, are standard/recommended readings in relevant college courses in the U.S., Canada, the Caribbean, and Latin America.

Awards and Honors

- Presidential Scholars Award for Excellence in Teaching
- National Endowment for the Arts
- Honores de Mérito: Asociación Nacional de Profesores de Cultura e Historia Dominicanas
- Puffin Award for Fiction

Printed in the United States
By Bookmasters